SERENDIPITY

A Bayou Magic Novel

KRISTEN PROBY

Ampersand Publishing, Inc.

Serendipity
A Bayou Magic Novel
By
Kristen Proby

SERENDIPITY

A Bayou Magic Novel

Kristen Proby

Cover Design: By Hang Le

Published by Ampersand Publishing, Inc.

Paperback ISBN: 978-1-63350-109-6

ACKNOWLEDGMENTS

There are some people that I need to thank, now that this series is all wrapped up.

A huge thank you goes out to Chelle Olson, who is not only my wonderful editor but also my friend. Thank you for helping me with all of the witchy things included in these three stories. More than that, you have my gratitude for loving these three sisters as much as I do.

To Jillian Stein, for all of the brainstorming, and for giving me Horace's name—no one could have come up with a creepier name for a serial killer. I love you.

The biggest thanks of all goes out to the readers who have come along with me on this new journey. For giving it a try and loving it enough to share it with your friends. The enthusiasm for my sister witches has been overwhelming. I think it's safe to say that this won't be the last time I write something in this genre.

Dear Reader,

Writing the Bayou Magic trilogy has been the thrill of my career so far. I've loved dabbling in the magic and dipping my toes into the thriller aspect of each story. I never thought that I'd combine a serial killer and witches into one series, but here we are.

And it's been absolutely amazing for me.

I know that these books are darker than what you have come to expect from me. While the romance is here, and there are plenty of moments to swoon, there is also a dark force afoot.

He is a serial killer, you know.

But there is also friendship and family, and a quest many lifetimes in the making. I hope you enjoy this last installment in the Bayou Magic series.

Now, go ahead and find a cozy spot, be sure to keep the lights on, and let me tell you a story...

xo,

Kristen

For Nora Roberts
Thank you for being my hero.

PROLOGUE

Daphne

Why won't Mama let me share a bedroom with my sisters? I'm scared. Of this house and all the things alive inside of it. I'm only nine, but I don't remember a time when I *wasn't* scared. When it gets dark outside, and Mama makes us go to bed, it's like the house comes to life—and tortures us.

Brielle sees the ghosts. They're shadows to her, and they follow her around, tormenting her. Millie feels the spirits and can see some of them, too. It happens all the time for them, not just at night. But it's worse in the dark—so much worse.

I can see the past when I touch things, feel how a person felt when they held whatever I am. I can see the spirits too, but only when I'm in direct contact with things. I try to be careful not to touch stuff, but it's impossible. I have to sit. I need to walk on floors and open doors. Eat. Play.

Brielle says there are other people like us, those who might be able to help us, but Mama won't let us talk about it. She beats us if she hears us whispering about it.

I wince when I turn over in bed. My arm still hurts from where Mama shook me this morning. I didn't want to use the bowl she put in front of me because Daddy used to use it, and all I see is anger. Meanness. Hate.

I tried to tell her, but she just hurt me.

My bed hurts me, too. The springs are coming through the mattress even though I put a blanket down to try and make it softer. Brielle's bed is better. And, sometimes, I sneak into her room so I can sleep with her.

I know he's in here with me. He thinks it's funny to watch me sleep, to make me scared. He did it when he was alive, too. I try to keep my eyes closed, to ignore him, but it's hard.

I crack them open and let out a yelp before I slam my hand over my mouth to stop the sound.

His face is inches from mine. His eyes shine in the dark, and his teeth are dirty and crooked. He's big and hairy and horrible.

Oh, God. Oh, God. Oh, God.

I fling the dirty blankets back and run for the door, easing it open and praying that Mama doesn't hear me. And then I hurry as fast as I can down the hall into Brielle's room.

"Come on," she whispers and holds up her blankets for me. I slip in next to her and cling to her, shivering. "What happened?"

"He was in my face," I whisper back and bury my nose in her neck. "He was smiling in that horrible way he does. It scares me."

"I know." She rubs my back. She's only fourteen, but she's an adult in all the ways that matter. She takes care of Millie and me. Someday, when she's eighteen, she's going to take us out of here so we never have to come back.

I wish that was today.

I wish it with all my heart.

"Millie's coming," Brielle whispers.

"How do you know?"

"I just do."

The door opens again, and Millie hurries to the bed, joining us under the covers.

"Daddy?" I ask her.

"Why won't he leave?" she whimpers. "Why won't he just leave?"

"Because he's mean," Brielle replies softly. "Now, stay quiet. We don't want Mama to find us in here together, remember?"

We go quiet, huddled together in the bed, listening to the house around us—all of its creaks and moans. Footsteps.

A door shuts down the hall.

"That's not Mama," Millie says and buries her face in

my hair. "Not Daddy, either."

"Who is it?" I ask her.

"I don't know. Never seen this one before."

I chew on my lip. "Why are there more? So many more."

"I don't know," Brielle says. "Maybe Daddy's bringing them here from the other side."

My eyes fill with tears as we hear the footsteps growing closer.

"Make it stop."

"I'M JACKSON PRUITT."

This boy, lean with dark hair and eyes, stands taller than me by at least half a foot. He has big hands. Men usually scare me. I don't trust them.

But Jackson's eyes are kind, and when I take the hand he offers to shake, I feel...warm.

"Daphne," I reply softly. "Daphne Landry."

"Millie's younger sister," he says with a smile, and I nod.

Since Brielle moved us out of Mama's house, it's safe to talk about our gifts. Millie found an actual *coven* to be a part of. Like, she's a real witch! That's still crazy to me. And she said that we're all invited to come and meet the people she knows. Millie says they're really nice.

And so far, she's been right.

"Yeah, Millie's my sister," I reply. I hate that I'm so shy. I wish I could talk to people easily like Brielle can, but I always feel awkward.

"Is this your first time here?" he asks. We're at Miss Sophia's house for a Halloween party.

No, that's not right. An All Hallow's Eve party. It's Samhain. What the witches call their new year. And there are supposedly all sorts of fantastical things about the night.

I nod and bite my lip. "I guess I'm kind of nervous."

"Oh, you don't have to be nervous," he assures and leads me over to a table where a black cauldron sits, full of smoking liquid. "Want a drink?"

"What is that?"

He laughs and ladles some. "It's punch. It's just fun to put it in here like it's a magical brew or something."

"Oh, okay."

I take a sip and blink in surprise. It's fruity and delicious.

"I know we just met and everything," Jackson says and wipes the palm of his hand on his jeans. "And you might run away when I say this, but I think you're the prettiest girl I've ever seen in my life."

Wow. No one's ever said *that* to me before.

"Gonna run?"

"No." I smile and then laugh a little. I'm still nervous, but if he thinks I'm pretty, I guess I can relax a bit. "Thanks for saying that. You're handsome, too."

And when he touches me, it's as if I've known him

for a long time.

"I'm going to marry you someday," he says with so much confidence, it makes me laugh in surprise.

"I'm only seventeen," I remind him.

"I said *someday.*" He nudges me with his shoulder. "I'm a patient guy. And I'm only eighteen myself, so we have lots of time."

I DON'T KNOW how I'm going to tell him. How does a person cut the one they love the most so deep? This will leave a scar forever.

The only man who's ever loved me. The first man I've given my love and trust to.

I may be young and not yet old enough to order a drink on Bourbon Street. I may still have a lot to learn about my gifts and how I walk through life with the hand Fate dealt me. But I know without a single doubt in my mind that Jackson Pruitt is meant for me. He's my soulmate—the other half of my heart.

And what I have to tell him will hurt him. It could change what we have between us forever.

"I'd rather cut my eyes out," I mutter with a sigh. I pace the living room of the apartment I share with my two older sisters in the French Quarter, waiting for Jack to come and get me for our date.

I haven't told anyone what I saw.

That's not new to me. I see so much, *all the time*,

that I keep most of it to myself. Talking about the things I see usually only scares people.

Not Brielle and Millie, of course. We've spoken about our gifts among the three of us our entire lives. But others—classmates and co-workers—would only be scared if I talked about the horrible things I see. It's hard enough to make friends as it is.

But when I met Jack, I just knew. Something moved in me, *through* me, as soon as I looked into his brown eyes. Some recognition. I knew that not only would he change my life, but he'd also *be* my life.

He knocks on the door. I hurry to open it and am swept up in his arms, his mouth on mine as he shuts the door behind us.

"I missed you," he murmurs against my lips.

His brown eyes are hot as he looks at me, but I see they still carry sadness in them.

"Same here. Jack, we have to talk."

"About dinner? Because I'm starving."

"No, not that." I smile. Jack's always hungry. I guess that goes with the territory of being so young. "We need to talk about your dad."

All humor flees from his face, and his brows draw together. "No, we don't."

"We really do," I insist and reach for his hand. Unfortunately, I regret the touch because I can feel his emotions.

Grief. Irritation. Weariness.

Jack's the only one I can read this way. Usually, only

objects tell me stories, not people.

"Let's sit down."

Jack's dad died two weeks ago. That's bad enough all by itself, but Jack also lost his mother after a long battle with cancer four weeks before that.

My love has known more heartache in the last year than any one person should.

"I saw something," I begin and take a deep breath. I always expect him to smirk or turn away from me, but he never does.

He loves me—gifts and all.

It doesn't hurt that he also has powers and was raised with the craft.

I feel my lips tremble, but I press them together as he takes my hands in his.

"Are you okay, Daph?"

I shake my head. "No. I'm not. And you won't be either after I tell you this."

His eyes narrow. "What happened? Did someone hurt you? Did you touch something? Damn it, Daph, you know to keep your shields up."

"It's not that," I hurry to assure him. "Do you remember last week, when we were at your house, and I sat in your dad's chair?"

"Sure."

I bite my lip. *Everything* in me screams not to tell him. This could change everything. I don't know how I know that, I just do.

"Well, you asked me if I saw anything, and I said no.

But that was a lie, Jack. I was so surprised, so taken aback, that I couldn't say anything then. But I have to tell you."

He narrows his eyes. "Okay, tell me."

"Your dad didn't die of natural causes like the medical examiner said."

"They did an autopsy, Daph."

"I know." I swallow again. "Jack, your dad killed himself. In that chair. He was thinking about how much he missed your mom and how he knew you'd be okay because you have Oliver and the rest of the coven—and me, of course. He just wanted to be with her."

"No." Jack shakes his head and stands from the couch, pacing away from me. "You saw it wrong."

I feel the tears start, just as I feel the chasm between us beginning to grow.

"I didn't see it wrong."

And, worst of all, it's *my* fault.

"I would have known," he insists, his voice hard. "You know that. I see shit, Daph, whether I want to or not. If he was going to die, I would have known."

"Maybe not. Maybe you're too close to him. Maybe he worked a spell and blocked you so you wouldn't stop him."

"This is *bullshit*." Jack's chin trembles, and I want to rush to him and wrap my arms around him.

But I know I'm not welcome.

"I'm so sorry, Jackson. So, so sorry."

"It's a lie. It's a hateful lie. Why would you say this

to me, Daphne? If you want to end it, just say so. You don't have to run me off like this. Put this kind of bull-shit in my head."

I shake my head in denial. "I wouldn't do that to you. I love you too much. This is killing me, Jack."

"Love?" He laughs—a humorless, horrible sound. "This isn't love. It's cruel."

I can't look at him. I can't watch the change unfolding right in front of my eyes.

I turn my back to him and cross my arms over my chest, suddenly feeling so cold, it's like I'll never be warm again.

"I promise you, it's not a lie. And I'm not trying to hurt you. You have the right to know what really happened."

"I want no part of this." His voice is low and ragged as he breathes hard with anger and grief. "I can't do this, Daphne."

I glance into the mirror across the room and watch as Jack gives me one last look, our eyes meeting in the reflective glass for a moment. And then he turns and walks away.

The door closes, and his footsteps fade down the steps.

I hang my head in my hands and let the tears come. Goddess, it hurts. It feels like my heart will never mend.

When I brush the tears away and look up again, I catch my reflection in the mirror—and stop cold.

I have no eyes.

CHAPTER ONE

Jackson

"What's on your plate today?"

I glance over as Oliver joins me on his screened-in porch, a steaming mug of coffee in his hand. He sits in the cushioned seat next to me and takes a sip.

"I have to go see Daphne today."

He's quiet for a moment as he watches butterflies and bumblebees flitting around his garden. Oliver is the closest thing to a father I've had since my parents died. He's my godfather. He was my dad's best friend and has been a part of my life since the day I was born.

I trust few people more than I do Oliver.

And it shames me that I've stayed away for as long as I have. I should have come home to New Orleans more often. I should have checked in with him—made more of an effort.

"You were angry," he says softly and then turns those wise brown eyes to me.

"Reading my mind again?" I sigh and sip the last of my coffee. "Yeah. I was angry."

"I don't feel the anger in you as much."

I shake my head. "Worry. I'm worried now. And ready to do what needs to be done to be with Daphne."

"Won't be easy."

I slide my gaze his way, studying the gray that slipped into his dark hair while I was gone. He has a few more wrinkles in his dark skin, and he moves a little slower than he used to.

And being with him makes me more comfortable than I've felt in *years*.

"If it were easy, it wouldn't be worth it." I set down my mug and lean forward, resting my elbows on my knees. "You know what's coming."

"I do," he agrees. "Doesn't matter what I know—or what anyone else knows for that matter. It's what *you're* going to do about it. What the six of you are gonna do."

"Yeah." I blow out a breath and check the time. "Hell, *you* know what's going to happen, but I don't understand it at all. I need answers. She should be at her shop. I'll go get this whole thing started."

"Be patient," Oliver warns me.

"Never been good at that." Still, I smile and pat Oliver on the shoulder before walking through the house to gather my keys and wallet and then make my way out to my car.

I was supposed to leave town a couple of weeks ago, to start a new job in Idaho. Now that I'm out of the

Army and its war zones and no longer moving all the time, it's time to lay down roots somewhere.

But when it was time to go, I just couldn't do it. I couldn't leave Louisiana in the rearview mirror.

I couldn't leave *Daphne.*

I drive through the city to the little antique shop she owns on the edge of the French Quarter. Reflections is a beautiful place, stuffed to the gills with everything from furniture to tiny tea sets. If it's old, Daph sells it.

Which is crazy to me. How does she not go insane? How can she touch so many things, experience what she must with each piece, and not lose her mind?

I grip the door handle to her store, and a premonition floods me. The edges of my vision go gray, and I'm suddenly *inside* the shop, looking up from the counter as a man walks into the store and crosses to me. His head is down, and I can't make out his face.

"May I help you?"

It's Daphne's voice, cheerful and ready to be of service to the customer.

But rather than answer, the guy looks up at her—at *me*—and he's missing his eyes.

I blink rapidly as the vision leaves me and swear under my breath.

Jesus.

I push through the door, and the little bell above it rings musically. She's diffusing clove and lemon oil for protection, and I can smell a hint of coffee in the air, as well.

"I'll be right with you," Daphne calls out from a room just behind the cash register. "Make yourself at home."

I don't say anything. I just push my hands into the pockets of my jeans and look around at what Daphne has done here.

It's impressive. According to Google and its two-hundred five-star ratings, she's built a business that is unique, fun, and boasts quality products—and she's not yet thirty.

I'm not surprised. Daphne wouldn't settle for anything less.

"So sorry to keep you waiting." She's out of breath as she hurries through the door. She has her red hair pulled back in a braid, but little strands of the auburn locks have worked themselves loose to frame her sweet face. Her cheeks are flushed, and her brow glistens with just a hint of sweat. "I had to wrestle an old trunk open. I don't think anyone's opened that sucker in fifty years, and—"

She comes to an abrupt stop when she sees that I'm her visitor.

Pleasure reaches her blue eyes first, and that fills my chest with hope. Unfortunately, guarded irritation quickly replaces it.

"Hi, Daph."

"Jack, I don't—"

"I know. You don't want to talk to me." I shake my head and turn from her so I don't rush over to her and wrap my arms around her. God, I've missed her. And she's as beautiful now, maybe even more so, than the first day I met her. "I know. But I need to talk to you, and you've been avoiding me like the damn plague."

"I've made it a habit to avoid unpleasant things."

Her toothy grin is anything but humorous.

"Point taken." Regret suddenly fills me. I wish I'd handled things differently years ago. "I want to talk to you about Millie's reception."

Daphne's older sister, Millie, married Lucien several weeks ago, but their reception and party was just three days ago. I was surprised to receive an invitation, but when I thought it over, it made sense.

Millie's part of the coven that I grew up in. I've known her for a long time.

Something quite powerful ties us together, and because of that, we have a bond.

"What about it?" Daphne asks, and I see the fatigue in her eyes when she sighs.

"You saw what I did." I swallow and have to stop myself from reaching for her again when I see fear cloud her eyes. "You saw it."

"I don't know what you mean."

"Yes, you do."

She moves to walk past me, but I catch her elbow in my grasp. A vision immediately fills my mind.

Fire.

Wind.

Chaos.

Fear.

She pulls back and narrows her eyes at me.

"We don't have anything to say to each other, Jack."

"Yes, we do. And you damn well know it. You *know*," I insist and shove my hand through my hair. "Yes, I messed up years ago, and you'd rather see the back of me than be nice. I get it. But, damn it, something's happening. It's escalating, and I need you to talk to me. I can't keep you safe like this, not with you closing me out."

"And why, pray tell, would you want to keep me safe?" Her voice drips with sarcasm. "You don't even like me."

"That's not true." I love her so much it makes me ache. "You saw the vision at the party. Every single person, standing there as if in a trance, without their eyes."

She stumbles, and when she turns those hot eyes to me again, they're wide and full of fear.

"What did you say?"

"You heard me." I watch her swallow hard. "You saw it. You went pale, and your pulse was thrumming in your neck. *I* saw that. Do you think I don't notice those things?"

"Look." Daphne walks to a lamp and straightens the lampshade. Her lips twitch into a small smile at the touch. "You made it clear years ago that you don't want anything to do with me."

"And I've done nothing but try to talk to you for weeks. To ask you to listen. I know things, Daph. I've been seeing things for months now. And it's getting worse."

"You've always seen things." She waves her hand, dismissing me.

"No. I cut that part of myself off after I left New Orleans." I rub my hand over my lips in frustration. "I *had* to. Had to turn it all off."

"Why?"

"It doesn't matter. I bound it, but things, *visions*, are breaking through my shields, and I know it's no coincidence that it's *you* I see in them. Us. With your sisters and their husbands."

She's quiet for a long moment and then sighs deeply, lowering herself onto a small, purple sofa before rubbing her fingertips over her forehead as if she's trying to rub away a headache.

"I hoped for more time," she says at last.

"More time for *what*?" I cross to her but don't touch her. I know it wouldn't be welcome. "I was with you and the others at Witches Brew when it seemed all hell broke loose. And even though I wasn't invited to the Samhain ritual during the blue moon, I *know* something happened there."

"Did Oliver tell you?" she asks softly, but I can see in her eyes that she already knows the answer.

"No. I watched it all unfold in my head, Daph. And I know, deep down, that something's about to happen. Something big. I just don't know what it is."

She nods. "Okay. I guess, whether I like it or not, it's time. We had a whole year between what happened with Brielle and the mess with Millie. I hoped for the same."

"You have to tell me what's going on. I deserve to know, especially if it involves me."

"I hate that you're right." She stands and spares a glance for the couple who just walked into her shop. "But I can't do this here. I need to work. Let's meet at Witches Brew later tonight after Millie closes. We'll explain everything to you."

"I'll be there."

I turn to leave but then look back at her. "It's not true, you know. What you said."

She quirks a brow.

"I don't dislike you. You're the only woman I've ever loved, Daphne. That hasn't changed."

"Excuse me?" a middle-aged man with silver hair interrupts. "Can I ask you a question about this umbrella stand?"

Daphne's eyes don't leave mine as she answers him. "Of course. I'll be right with you."

"I'll let you work." I wink at her and move toward the door. "I'll see you tonight."

I leave the shop and walk to my car. When I glance

into the big front window of Reflections, I see Daphne still watching me.

"I KNOW WE'RE LATE," Brielle announces as she and her husband, Cash, rush into Millie's café. Cash locks the door behind them.

I'm sitting at the coffee counter, taking them all in. Millie and Lucien move, touch, and look at each other as though they've been a couple for many years—certainly longer than the few months I know they've been together. Brielle laughs with Daphne as they chat about their days.

The three sisters couldn't be more different—at least physically. Brielle, the eldest, has dark hair with blue eyes and a curvy figure. Millie is tall and willowy with long, blonde locks. And my Daphne has that fiery, curly red hair and a petite body that makes my mouth water.

But despite the lack of resemblance, they share an unbreakable bond—a fierce loyalty and love.

"It's good to see you," Brielle says and pats me on the shoulder. I glance warily at Daphne.

The last time Daph saw me with Brielle, she was *livid*. Felt betrayed.

And that only added fuel to the fire of her animosity toward me.

"You, too."

"I'm glad you're here," Millie says to me as she wipes down the counter.

I glance at Lucien, who just grins and leans over to kiss his bride on the cheek.

"First, why don't you tell us all why you've been so insistent on speaking with Daphne?" Brielle suggests. "Aside from the personal stuff you share, of course. Not that we don't want to hear about that, but it's probably none of our business."

"Definitely none of your business," Cash says, earning a glare from his wife.

"Since I don't know Cash well, I'll start back a ways." I wipe my hand over my face and test my shields.

They're strong.

"I grew up in the coven, just like Lucien."

"You're a witch?" Cash asks.

"Not a practicing one, no. Not for a long while, anyway. My gift was always premonitions. I was able to see things before they happened."

"You could win the lottery with that," Cash suggests, and I laugh.

"It doesn't really work that way, unfortunately. It's more visions of events before they happen. Have you ever had a sense of déjà vu? Like you think to yourself, *I've done this before*."

"Of course."

"We all have a little precognition in us," Lucien says before taking a sip of coffee.

"We're having coffee?" Daphne demands. "Give me."

Millie gets to work filling a cup for her sister.

"Precognition is my thing." I stand, shove my hands into my pockets, and pace the café. "Or, it was. I've worked hard to block that part of myself for quite a long time. I was in the Army. Let me just tell you, it sucks ass when you know in advance when your buddies are going to die in action."

"Jesus," Cash breathes.

"I built shields, worked a couple of spells. I even spent a whole evening on the phone with Miss Sophia, and she helped me, too. I haven't seen anything in *years.*"

"Until recently," Lucien guesses.

"Until a few months ago," I agree. "And no matter what I do, I can't block it. It's fire and brimstone. Despair. Pain. It's the scariest shit I've ever seen in my damn life, and trust me when I say, I've seen some shit."

"Do you see the outcome?" Millie asks, sounding almost desperate.

"No. And I don't know if what I'm seeing is what *will* happen or if it's what *may* happen. I asked Miss Sophia about it, and she said it's not for her to tell me. I don't know what happened on Halloween night, not exactly. But I can tell you that I was drenched in sweat all evening, couldn't catch my breath, and then, suddenly, it was just...*gone.*"

"Fascinating," Lucien says.

"I know one thing," I continue. "In every vision, I see Daphne. I see the six of us. And it's damn frustrating that I don't know *why*. I've been trying to get Daph to speak to me, but we have...history."

The woman I love frowns down into her coffee.

"It's escalating quickly," Brielle murmurs.

"*What* is?" I demand. "What in the hell is going on?"

"A battle a millennium in the making," Lucien informs me. "We've done this over many lifetimes—and we've always lost."

For the next hour, the five of them fill me in on apparitions, dead girls, epic fights. A serial killer.

Past lives.

An evil father, who I already knew about. And their mother, escaping the terrors of their scary home in the bayou and healing.

"We've defeated him twice before," Millie finishes. "But not for *good*. Not forever. We can't cast him out without the six of us being together."

"Why didn't you just call me on Halloween if you knew that was the case?" I demand. "This could be *done*."

"It wasn't time," Lucien says simply.

"So, what now?" I ask. "How do we find him and defeat him?"

"He hasn't started manifesting himself yet," Cash reminds us. "We can't do anything until he makes the first move."

My gaze whips to Daphne's. "You didn't tell them?"

"Tell us what?" Brielle asks, coming to attention.

Daphne just watches me. "Tell us *what?*" Brielle demands again.

"Something happened at the reception," Daphne says softly. "I was in the restroom, avoiding G.I. Joe over there."

I grin and rock back on my heels. If she's trying to avoid me, it's because she still feels something.

I can work with that.

"When I walked out of the bathroom and came around the house to the tent where everyone was, it was still. Dead quiet. The guests were facing away from me, but they suddenly turned around to stare at me—and they were all missing their eyes."

"Jesus," Cash mutters.

"Oh, Daphne," Millie says and hurries around the counter to hug her sister. "Why didn't you say something?"

"Because it was your *wedding reception*," Daphne reminds her. "What would you have had me do? Interrupt the fun and say, *'Oh, by the way, an evil serial killer is terrorizing me today?'*"

"Yeah," Brielle says, nodding. "That's exactly what you should have said."

"At the very least," Lucien adds, "you should have called us all together the next morning so we could talk it through."

"Well, I came out of it—the trance or whatever—and it didn't happen again," Daphne replies.

"But I saw it, too," I say.

Five pairs of eyes turn to me.

"I was watching for Daphne, and when I saw her stop so abruptly and noticed the fear in her eyes, I looked back, and I saw it, too. And the shittiest thing is, that was one of my visions. But I didn't know until I was in that exact spot that *that's* what I'd seen."

"Before that day, when was your vision?" Millie asks.

I blink, thinking back. "Oh, geez, it must have been...a week before? Maybe a little more."

"It's starting much earlier this time," Brielle says.

"Makes sense," Lucien adds. "He's angry. Question: have you two seen the same things in the past?"

"No, I have precognition, and Daph sees the past. It's never overlapped before."

"Wow," Cash exclaims. "This is intense."

"I need more coffee," Daphne says and walks behind the counter to brew a cup. "And why didn't I realize that? Why didn't it occur to me that we've never seen the same thing before?"

"Because you're too worried about me," I reply and grin when she narrows her eyes. "You're not objective when it comes to me."

"Arrogant much?" She lifts an eyebrow.

"Is it any wonder that I'm crazy about you?"

"He's right," Lucien adds. "It didn't occur to you because you're too worried about the personal side of things. But we all have to remember to keep our eyes open and make a note of everything because there are no coincidences or accidents. What happened to you two at our reception was purposeful and meant to throw you both off."

"So, what do we do?" I demand. "How do we end this fucker? I won't have him hurt Daphne—or any of you, for that matter. This needs to be over."

"As frustrating as it is, we wait," Lucien says. "This phase is just beginning. We have to wait."

"We need to recharge the stones in Daphne's shop and at her apartment," Millie says, making a mental list. "Cast protection spells daily."

"Daily?" Daphne questions. "I don't need you to do that."

"Yes." I cross my arms over my chest and narrow my eyes at her. "You do. We will."

Daphne looks as if she might yell at me, but Brielle speaks again before that can happen.

"I think we should all stay in the same place," she says. "We're stronger together."

"We have plenty of space," Millie offers. "Our house is big, so we won't be on top of each other."

"No," Daphne says, shaking her head. "Absolutely, not. I'm not going to let him run me out of my home. I have a business. A *life*. And since all he's done so far is try to scare me, I'm staying home."

"*Now* is when you decide to let your stubbornness rule?" Brielle demands.

"I'm not being unreasonable," Daphne says with a sigh. "He hasn't done anything that we know of besides these parlor tricks."

"I'll be keeping an eye on you." My voice is stern, leaving no room for argument or discussion. "From here on out until this is finished."

"We all will," Cash says. "And the *second* something happens, you call us."

"Trust me," Daphne says. "I'm scared. I'm not going to do anything stupid. I'm not going to put any of you in jeopardy."

"Are you planning to drop your shields?" Millie asks me.

"I thought about it," I admit. "If it will help me see things more clearly."

"No." Lucien shakes his head. "If he's able to get into your head with your protections intact, I can't even imagine what he could do if you weren't protected. Keep them up."

"And what do we do now?" Daphne asks, but Lucien already answered that question.

He smiles patiently at his sister-in-law. "We wait."

CHAPTER TWO

Daphne

"Hello, little girl."

"I'm not *a little girl*," I insist. But he just smiles bigger, showing me those crooked teeth.

I'm standing in the middle of a sidewalk in a courtyard. I see grass all around me, and he's standing in front of a fountain, his arms crossed over his chest, his eyes pinned to mine. Yet, he remains unblinking—and he's creepy as fuck.

Yep, that's Daddy.

I can't lift my feet. When I'm finally able, I move as if I'm trudging through mud. Slow and clumsily.

"You can't run away from me, little girl," he snarls. "I'm always nearby. Always watching. You're my *little girl.*"

"I'm not a little girl!" I yell in frustration, but he doesn't even flinch.

"An ungrateful little girl, that's what you are."

I want to kill him. I want to run over and rip that slimy smile off his disgusting face.

But I can't move.

I sit up in bed and swipe my hand over my face. I'm sweating. My heart is racing.

I glance over to check the time.

Three o'clock on the nose.

The witching hour.

I hate the middle of the night. Even after we escaped the house in the bayou, the nights still scare me. I usually keep a light on in my apartment, but I scowl when I realize it's out.

I slip my feet into my slippers, wrap my robe around me, and pad into the bathroom, flipping on the light. Weird. I *know* that it was on when I went to bed.

I use the restroom and then wash my hands, drying them before glancing up.

I yelp and blink, and then it's gone.

"I'm losing my mind," I mutter and will my heart rate to slow down. "I did *not* just see my father in the mirror. He's gone. Long gone."

I just wish I could make my subconscious get the memo.

I'M SO *TIRED*. Because even though I went back to bed, I still had dreams.

I've been sleeping well, but the dreams that plague me are awful. Too real. Full of horrible memories of living in the bayou with my sisters, victims of a possessed mother, and the spirit of our evil father.

He's been coming to me in dreams regularly—not just last night. Our daddy. And it's as terrifying now as it was when I was small and helpless.

I'm neither of those things any longer, and yet, the man who sired me continues to torment me.

I haven't told my sisters yet. They'll be angry that I didn't confide in them, but I don't want to scare them. We've had enough fear over the past year—hell, in our entire lifetimes.

I couldn't bear to add more fear to their lives.

I rub my hand over my face and pad into the kitchen, making a beeline for the coffee maker.

My precious, wonderful coffee maker.

But before I can turn it on, a knock sounds at my door.

"I can't be expected to be nice to people before I'm caffeinated," I mutter as I pad to the entrance of my apartment and open it to find Jack standing there, looking fresh and well-rested and just *sexy*. "Do you realize that it's, like, seven?"

"Good morning," he says with that grin that always makes my knees weak. "I brought you coffee."

He holds out the cup, and I snatch it away and take a long sip, not caring in the least that it's so hot it could boil pasta al dente.

"Need," I say with a grateful sigh, closing my eyes

and then reopening them to stare at him. Goddess, he's only gotten more handsome with age.

It's not fair.

"Can I come in?" he asks at last.

"Oh. Okay." I back away from the door and drop into a chair in the living room, pulling my feet up under me and savoring another long sip.

"Do you have any other clothes you can wear?"

I scowl and look down at my robe. "Why?"

"Because you're likely naked under there, and I'm a mortal man, Daph."

I don't move to cover the cleavage that shows thanks to the gaping robe lapel. I'm just that spiteful.

Instead, I raise a brow and take another sip of coffee.

"That would be a *no* then," he says with a deep sigh and shoves his hand through his hair.

"To what do I owe this visit and this delicious brew?" I ask.

"Just thought I'd stop by and see how you're doing."

"I'm fine, thanks. You don't have to hover, you know. Everything is fine."

Except my father is terrorizing me in my dreams again. No big deal.

"I told you that I'd be sticking close, keeping an eye out."

"That's very chivalrous of you." I suck down the last of the coffee, then stand and walk into the kitchen to brew some more. "Millie and Brielle are coming over tonight for a girls' night and to work some protection spells. We've already recharged the stones at Reflections. He can't come inside, Jack. I'm safe."

"Listen, it's no skin off your nose if I stick close."

"It's a free country," I mutter and will the coffee to brew faster.

"How much coffee do you drink in a day?" he asks.

"As much as humanly possible." I turn a steely stare at him. "And I haven't had enough this morning to throw you out on your ass. Yet."

"Good." He leans back and grins, his arms spread across the back of the couch. It's that cocky grin that always made me want to kiss the lips right off his face.

It would be so easy to fall in love with him once more. To soften and just *be* with him.

But he hurt me deeper than anyone ever has in my life, and I don't trust that he won't do it again.

"You know, when I met you, you were such a shy thing. Quiet and unsure. Even when things ended, you were quiet."

"I'm not loud now," I reply with a shrug. "But I *am* more confident."

"I like it," he says, watching me. "I liked you fine before, but you wear confidence well, Daph."

"I have to go see my mother today," I inform him and brush my hair off my neck, changing the subject. "With my sisters. And then we're coming back here for dinner. Girls' night, as I said."

"Good. I'm glad you won't be alone." His expression

sobers. "Is Ruth really doing well? From everything you told me back when we were together, she was a horrible person."

I doctor up a new cup of coffee, forgoing the potion Millie insisted I use, and return to my chair.

"Yeah, she is doing well. She was possessed by...*something*...for a long time. Held hostage in that house. We've been there a couple of times in the past year, and the paranormal activity has only gotten worse, Jack. It's full of spirits, shadows, and...*evil.* The house itself is falling apart. And my father is buried in the rose garden."

I shed the vision that fills my head every time I think of that place.

"What is it?" he asks.

"What is what?"

"Your eyes just went unfocused. You saw something. What was it?"

How can he still read me so well?

I blow out a breath and then decide: *What the hell?*

"When we went to the house to find our grand-mother's grimoire, Mama led me out to the garden. Said she wanted to show me her roses or something. We were alone because Millie and Cash were upstairs, looking for the book, and Brielle stopped to look at something in the house. Anyway, she led me into the backyard. The rose bushes were *ridiculous*, Jack. As if they were grown with fertilizer on steroids. I reached out and touched a blossom.

"Now, I'd been *so* careful throughout the entire house because...well, you know."

He nods, his eyes narrowed, and I keep going.

"Anyway, she was rattling on about how she killed my father. And I touched the bloom. Suddenly, it was as black as a moonless night, and my father's voice started cackling in my head—an evil, awful laugh. I hadn't seen him in years, not since Miss Sophia helped us get rid of him with a spell. But he's buried in that garden, Jack. And his spirit is still very much in that house."

"Jesus," he murmurs and presses his fingertips to his eyes. "I'm so damn sorry, Daph."

"I'm fine," I assure him, even though not much about my childhood was *fine*. "I'm used to all of this. It's happened forever."

"And that just pisses me right off," he says, but his voice is soft. "No one deserves to be taunted the way the three of you have been."

"Four," I remind him. "Mama got the worst of it. But she's doing great now. Unbeknownst to all of us, we found out Mama's a witch."

"What? I thought she punished you guys if you talked about those kinds of things."

"Oh, she did. Well, whatever possessed her did. But we discovered that not only was she a witch before, she was also a member of Miss Sophia's coven."

His eyes fly to mine. "*Our* coven?"

"That's right."

"And no one did anything? Said anything?"

"Miss Sophia said that Mama was always a little... difficult. Moody. Probably from being married to my dad." I shrug. "She didn't know what was happening at the house."

"No one ever said anything to me about your mom," he mutters in confusion.

"They'd probably tell you that it wasn't for them to talk about. Or that it wasn't time." I roll my eyes. "This mystical stuff is damn frustrating."

He shrugs and then nods. "Yeah, I can see that. Still, it's all fascinating."

"Thanks for the coffee. And for checking in." I stand and straighten my robe, enjoying a brief moment of female satisfaction when Jackson's pupils dilate. "But I have to get over to Brielle's so we can go see Mama."

"Yeah, I have places to be, as well. I was going to ask you to dinner, but since you're spending time with your sisters, I'll save that."

"Jack." I sigh as I walk him to the door. "We aren't dating."

"Who said anything about dating?" He winks, flashes that knee-weakening smile, and then he's gone.

I shut the door and look back into the room. "Why does he have to be so damn charming?"

"Do you think Mama's ready to get out of the hospital?" Millie asks as we drive to the place Mama's been living since she was removed from the house in the bayou.

"She's stronger than ever," Brielle reminds our sister. "She's been able to go out and enjoy things. So many spells protect her at this point, nothing's going to get at her."

"We hope," I whisper and turn my car into the parking lot of the hospital. "Let's see how this goes."

My sisters and I have held a grudge for years. Like Miss Sophia, we had no idea that our mother was possessed. We just thought she was awful. That she was content to live in that mean old house.

But we've come to realize that our mother is not the mean old woman we thought she was. Since being free of the possession, she's mourned the years she lost with us, and she's been kind and helpful.

The type of mother all three of us needed from the start.

I find a place to park, and we make our way through security and up to Mama's floor.

We find her sitting in a chair by the window, reading a book, with a soft smile on her face. She's tall, with long, blonde hair like Millie's, but Mama's is streaked with gray. Her face is free of makeup, but she's wearing her mother of pearl pendant. I notice someone painted her fingernails a pretty light pink.

When she looks up at us, her face transforms with a bright smile.

"Oh, my girls. How wonderful to see you."

We take turns kissing her cheek and then take our seats.

"How are you feeling, Mama?" Brielle asks.

"Oh, just fine," Mama replies and reaches out to pat Brielle's hand. "I'm doing just fine."

"You look great," I say. "I heard a rumor that they might spring you out of here soon."

Mama's smile fades. "Yes, so they've said."

"Doesn't that make you happy?" Brielle asks.

"I feel conflicted," Mama admits. "I know I can't stay here forever. And, honestly, it's not the most comfortable of places. It's not awful," she rushes to assure us. "But it is a hospital."

"Exactly," Millie says, nodding.

"But, girls, where will I go? I don't have a home anymore."

"We have some thoughts on that," Brielle says and holds Mama's hand. "We would like to build you a little cottage near Miss Sophia's house."

Mama's eyes widen. "I couldn't ask you to do that."

"You're not asking," I reply. "Miss Sophia has plenty of property, and she offered a little piece of it to us to build the cottage. You'll be near her. Near the coven."

Mama brushes a tear off her cheek. "I don't deserve any of this. After the way I behaved, and how you girls were treated—"

"That wasn't *you*," Millie reminds her. "That wasn't your fault, and we know it. It'll take a little time to build the house, but you're welcome to stay with Miss Sophia until it's finished."

"I don't want to put her out."

"She insisted," I reply. "It'll only be for a few months."

"I don't know what to say. Thank you very much. I love you three more than I can ever tell you. I'm just gutted by what I've remembered. It's only bits and pieces, but even that much absolutely horrifies me. I'll spend the rest of my days making it up to you."

"We love you, too," Brielle says, and I know what she's thinking.

None of us ever thought we'd be here, telling our mother that we love her.

"I ALREADY HAVE some furnishings picked out for Mama's new place," I inform the girls as we carry pizza into my apartment. "Things set aside for her."

"Good, because we'll leave the bulk of the décor up to you," Brielle says. "You have such an eye for it."

I grin and think of the gorgeous yellow velvet sofa I chose for her. With the right pillows and accent pieces, it'll be perfect.

"First thing's first," Millie says as she bites into a slice of the pepperoni pizza. "I have a few protection spells to cast, and I brought you some fresh crystals for all four corners."

I eat my dinner and grin as Millie flits around, casting spells and setting crystals. She even steps outside for a minute. When she reopens my door, I see blood on it.

"Uh, Mill, you don't need to bleed for me."

"Just a little." She winks, takes another bite of pizza, and then wanders back to my bedroom.

"Do you ever have the urge to join the coven?" I ask Brielle.

"No," she says, shaking her head. "I don't mean that to sound harsh. I know that I have magic in me. And I don't hate it. I'm also grateful that all of the witches have pitched in to help without batting an eye and helped us defeat Ho—*him*—twice. They're great people, and I consider them friends.

"But I just don't have any interest in the magical side of things, you know? I'm not afraid of it. It's just not my thing."

"I understand." I chew my pizza thoughtfully. "I've thought about going back to it."

A few years after Millie joined her coven, I dabbled a bit in magic. It's how I met Jackson. I enjoyed it. I'm not a particularly powerful witch, but I like the community aspect of it.

"You should," Brielle says.

"Should what?" Millie asks, and I relay our conversation. "You're always welcome. You know that. Both of you. You *are* witches. Whether you join a coven or not is completely up to you."

"I know," Brielle says with a smile. "And I appreciate it."

"I'll keep thinking about it," I add. "Now, are you all done casting my protective bubble?"

"Yeah. It's a strong spell and should keep you perfectly safe while you're here or at your shop. He can't get through it. Can't terrorize you here."

Can you do the same about our father?

But I don't voice it aloud.

Brielle's eyes narrow as she glances at my window.

"What?"

She tips her head to the side. "Have you always had a little girl who looks in your window?"

"Oh, that?" I wave my hand in dismissal. "Yeah. I don't see her, but I walked barefoot across my balcony one day after I first moved in here, and I felt her. She used to live here."

"We can help her move on," Millie offers.

"No," Brielle says, shaking her head. "She looks over things. Keeps an eye out. Don't send her away."

"I don't mind if she stays." I reach for another slice of pizza and try to sound nonchalant. "Hey, Mill, do you have a sleeping potion that can keep a person from dreaming?"

"Sure." Millie pours us all glasses of wine. "Do you want to swing into the café tomorrow? I'll give it to you."

"That would be great," I admit. "I'm sleeping fine,

but my dreams are all over the place, so I'm always tired."

"That's exhausting," Millie says. "I have something that will help."

"Great, thanks." I sip my wine. "Jackson came by today."

"Tell us everything." Brielle takes a drink. "Did you get naked?"

"Of course, not." I roll my eyes.

"Oh, come on, Daph," Millie says. "He's still hot. Maybe hotter. Are you telling us that you feel *nothing* for him?"

"No, I'm not saying that at all. I'm as attracted to him today as I was when I met him at seventeen."

"Then why won't you give him a chance?"

"Who says he *wants* a chance?" I ask.

"Oh, come on. Jack's still into you." Brielle points at me. "You're just being stubborn."

"I'm protecting myself," I admit. "He hurt me. No, he *destroyed* me. And if I let him in now, he could do it again. I don't think I'd survive it a second time."

"Maybe stay wary, but also let him kiss you," Millie suggests. "Because he *wants* to kiss you."

"Stop reading his mind."

"I haven't read him," Millie insists. "You don't have to be psychic to know that man wants to get his lips on you—and probably other things, too."

I laugh and fill our wine glasses again. "Well, he can keep his lips to himself."

"That's so *boring*," Millie insists.

"Then here's to boring." I hold my glass up in cheers. "Just because you two are all about hearts and flowers doesn't mean I have to follow suit."

"We want you to be happy, Daph," Brielle says.

"I am happy." I smile, but I know they can see through me. See the lie.

They always do.

"I'm totally happy."

CHAPTER THREE
Jackson

"What a lovely surprise." Miss Sophia opens the door of her cabin in the bayou and gestures for me to come inside. "I just put on some tea."

"At six in the morning, I'm usually a coffee man." I smile down at her as she closes the door and gestures again for me to follow her. "But you always make a mean cup of tea."

"It'll be good for you."

"Are you going to add a protection potion like Millie does?" I ask and lean on the doorjamb of her tidy kitchen as she pours the cups.

"No, she has you covered there," Miss Sophia replies with a wink.

"I'm sorry if I woke you."

"You didn't. I knew you were coming, so I was up early, brewing this tea." She passes me the cup and offers me honey and milk, but I take it black. "You're worried."

"Yeah." I push my hand through my hair and sit across the table from Miss Sophia, who just sips from her mug and watches me with wise, blue eyes. "He's going to try to hurt her."

"Of course."

She doesn't even play coy, asking who *he* is.

I love that about her.

"How do I stop it?"

She sips again and watches me over the rim. "You know I can't tell you that."

"No, I don't know it. If you know how to resolve all of this, why won't you just tell us so we can get rid of this murdering bastard for good?"

"Because that's not how it's meant to be." She smiles when I curse under my breath. "Ah, Jackson, I did miss you. And I'm glad that you're home now, where you should be."

"I feel like I've come into a game at the end of the fourth quarter and haven't warmed up. But I'm still expected to throw the winning pass."

"If you'd joined the others sooner, it wouldn't have been the right time. Not right for you, nor right for Daphne. Each sister had to complete her quest before it was Daphne's turn."

"*My* turn."

She doesn't answer. She simply smiles.

"The others told me that I'm one of the six."

"Oh, you've already met with them then? How lovely."

"No." I stand and pace near the table. "No, nothing about this is *lovely*."

"You're right. But I'm happy to hear that you're working together. The sooner, the better."

"Horace has already started," I say and turn to find her serene smile gone, and her sharp eyes narrowed.

"Tell me." Her voice is a whip.

I explain what Daphne and I both saw at the wedding reception. The one that was held just behind this house, out in a field where the coven performs sacred rites regularly.

"And I'm having visions," I admit.

It's not encouraging when her jaw drops.

"Jackson, the spells I cast to keep your visions away, everything we've done to prevent exactly that, are strong."

"And yet, here we are." I sit again and watch her grimly. "It seems the visions are going to happen, regardless. I thought of dropping my shields altogether so I could see better and protect Daphne, but Lucien said no."

"I agree with him," she says and stands to mix herbs, putting them into a little brown pouch. "I know that Millie is our hedgewitch, but I want you to take this tea and drink it. A cup every day."

She passes it to me, and I tuck it into my pocket.

"I need more information."

She sits once more and lets out a small sigh. I think this is the first time in my life I've ever seen Miss Sophia look conflicted.

"The answers you seek are in the other five. I'm not permitted to tell you what you want to hear, Jackson. Giving you too much information could be dangerous. But I'll say this: You must be careful. Stay aware. Take anything you see or feel with a grain of salt. Everything from here on out is important."

"Pay attention." I nod. "Yeah, well, it'll be hard not to. I won't let him hurt her."

She reaches across the table and takes my hand. "Child, being hurt is inevitable."

I shake my head, but before I can reply, the edges of my vision go gray, and I'm thrust into a vision.

Daphne. I'm looking at Daphne's apartment. Her door opens. She looks down with a scowl, picks up an envelope, and then screams.

"Jackson?"

"I have to get to Daphne. Damn it. I need to get to her now."

I stand and rush out of the cabin, driving faster through the bayou than anyone has any business going. Traffic through the French Quarter isn't crazy yet as most of the city is still asleep.

I run a red light and come to a screeching halt in front of Daphne's building. As I'm rushing up the walk, I see her door open.

"Daph!" I yell, catching her attention.

She blinks and then frowns at me. "What are you doing here?"

I run up the stairs to her balcony and see the envelope on the stoop.

Before she can look down and grab it, I snatch it up.

"What's that? Jack, this isn't funny."

"I had a vision." I'm panting like crazy from the adrenaline and running up the stairs. "Shit, Daph, I came all the way from Miss Sophia's."

I back her into her apartment.

"Okay, now you're freaking me out," she says. "You're as pale as a ghost."

The envelope pulses in my grasp as if it has a heartbeat.

"Give me the envelope." Her voice is perfectly calm. Her face clear of distress. She holds her hand out. "It's okay, Jack."

"I'm right next to you," I remind her. "I'm right *here*."

"Okay. We've got this."

I pass it to her, and she immediately scowls.

"Heartbeat?" I ask her.

"So weird," she mutters. "But everything about this is ridiculously weird."

On the back of the envelope, written in a chicken scratch that looks like something a six-year-old wrote, is one word: *DAPHNE.*

"I'm putting fingerprints all over this," she mutters. "Cash'll be pissed."

"Well, you have to see what's inside," I remind her.

She pulls out a photo.

A Polaroid.

In black and white, it's a picture of a woman staring straight into the camera—only her shoulders and head visible in the frame.

And her eyes are missing.

"Oh, my goddess," Daphne mutters and puts the photo facedown.

"There's a timestamp on it," I say and slip the image from her hands to study it. "Two-oh-eight in the afternoon. Today."

We look at each other.

"Today?" she asks. "It's only like seven in the morning."

"I think this means he's going to kill her this afternoon."

"But who is she?" Daphne takes the photo back from me. "Without her eyes, it's almost impossible to tell."

"Or the camera is broken. Or set on the wrong time."

"It's set on the wrong time," she confirms. "But on purpose. He's messing with me now, Jack. It's started."

I blow out a breath and reach for my phone.

"Who are you calling?"

"Your sisters. If you think we're not telling them about this—"

"I don't think that. I know we are." She sets the

photo and envelope on the table in front of her, watching them as if they might jump up and bite her. "I need to get dressed."

"Do that. I'll make the calls."

"Thanks." She stands to walk into her bedroom but stops and looks back at me with haunted eyes. "Thank you. I mean that."

"No need to thank me, sweets." I wink at her and toss her the arrogant grin I know she likes, just to lighten the mood and give her a second of normalcy.

But when she's out of the room, and Brielle answers her phone, I get serious again.

"Jack?" Brielle asks. "Are you okay?"

"It's started," I reply. "Everyone needs to come to Daphne's."

"We're on our way."

"WHAT HAPPENED?" Millie demands, the first in line as the four of them march into Daphne's apartment. Millie has a huge paper sack, and Lucien comes in right behind her with a tray of coffees.

Brielle has another tray.

"You brought breakfast?" Daphne asks in surprise.

"We have to eat," Cash says and bites into an apple fritter. "And you know she put all kinds of woo-woo protection stuff in all of this."

"It's a two-for," Brielle agrees. "Now, talk."

I explain my visit to Miss Sophia—the vision and racing over to Daph's.

"How did you know that it hadn't happened yet? Or that it wasn't happening as you saw it?" Cash asks.

"Because that's not how it works with me," I reply. "It's always precognition. I don't know how I knew it was *about* to happen right away. I just knew I had to get here."

"Then we found the envelope," Daphne says, picking up the story. "Brought it inside and opened it."

"Did *both* of you touch it?" Cash asks.

"Yeah." Daphne winces when Cash's eyes narrow.

"Have I taught you *nothing*?" he demands.

"I had to open it," Daphne replies. "And let me just say, I could have gone my whole life without seeing what was inside."

Cash puts on some gloves—ignoring the snickers from the rest of us at the sight of him carrying gloves around—and then reaches over to the table to pick up the envelope.

When he pulls out the photo, his face goes stone-cold.

"Son of a bitch."

"Oh, damn," Brielle mutters.

Millie and Lucien look at each other and seem to have some unspoken conversation.

"The timestamp," I point out.

Cash scowls again. "It hasn't happened yet."

"Wait, what?" Millie asks. "What do you mean?"

"Just that," Cash says. "The time on this photo is later today."

"He hasn't killed her yet," Lucien says.

"But she's missing her *eyes*," Daphne puts in.

"We're dealing with a supernatural entity," Millie reminds us all. "He can manipulate technology. But how is he doing this? Has he inhabited another body?"

"Has anyone spoken with Dahlia lately?" Brielle asks.

"Who's Dahlia?" I blink at the others, still feeling like I didn't do my homework.

It's damn frustrating.

"Dahlia was the witch Hor—*he* inhabited last time," Millie says with sadness in her blue eyes. "She sold her flower shop and moved to Miami. She's long gone."

"I don't blame her," Brielle mutters. "After what she went through, I'd move far away, too."

"I don't think he's possessed someone else," Lucien says, thinking it over. "I could be wrong, but that didn't exactly work out well for him the last time."

"How else can he kill people?" I demand. "How can he take pictures and drop them off here?"

"Good question," Millie says. "That's a damn good question. I need to consult the grimoires."

"I think we need to know who this woman is first. How do we get to her before he kills her?" Cash wonders.

"You won't find her," Lucien says, sorrow heavy in his voice. "If we've learned anything from the past year, it's that killing is what he does best. Better, even, than taunting our girls. It's his passion, the way gardening or painting is for others. Murder is his hobby, and he's damn good at it."

"Who is she?" Daphne mutters, examining the photo. "And why is it so hard to identify someone without their eyes?"

"I can run her through a database," Cash offers. "But it's not going to be fast. I'll narrow it down to anyone living in Louisiana with the attributes that we can make out, but as we all know, she could be a tourist."

"It can't be hopeless," I mutter. "Why else would he show us who he's going to kill?"

"Aside from the fact that he's a sick fuck?" Cash asks.

"Okay, point taken." We sit in silence for a moment. "He was able to get to Daph's doorstep. He walked right up here and left this on the mat."

"The protection spells are for *inside* the dwelling," Millie replies.

"Is it possible to put her in a bubble? If he can get to her door, he can look in the windows."

"I'm on the second floor," Daphne reminds me.

"And he's not a *man* anymore. Do you think he can't just float on up here and look inside?"

Daphne goes pale and swallows hard. "Well, that's a lovely thought. I'll never get naked again."

"He can't see inside," Millie rushes to assure us. "I

set that spell, as well. He can't see in. He can't hear what happens in here, either."

"Well, that's something, I guess." I reach over and take Daphne's hand, encouraged when she doesn't immediately pull away. "You *are* safe here, you know."

"Yeah. Sure." She blows out a breath. "I don't know what to do. I have to open the shop today, but I hate the idea of knowing that this poor woman is out there somewhere, going through Goddess knows what. And that she only has mere hours to live."

"Unfortunately, there's nothing you can do," Lucien says and rubs circles over Millie's back. "It's already been set in motion."

"I'll do what I can on my side of things," Cash says. "I'm taking this with me."

"Good." Daphne waves it away. "Get it out of here. I don't want to see it again."

"I'm going to Reflections with you," I inform Daphne. "I'm going to be stuck to you like glue for the foreseeable future."

"That's just silly—" she starts to object, but Brielle surprises her by speaking up.

"That's an excellent idea," Brielle says. "You shouldn't be alone, Daph. Even with all the protection spells in the world. We've learned the hard way that this maniac can manipulate and worm his way in where he's not wanted. It will make me feel so much better if Jackson sticks close."

"I don't need a babysitter," Daphne mutters, but she

doesn't argue. "Fine. You can be the muscle of the operation today. Some heavy pieces came in that I want on the showroom floor."

"It's always my pleasure to be the brawn to your brains."

Daphne rolls her eyes, and Lucien laughs.

"It's settled then," Millie says.

"I WANT THAT PLANTER OVER THERE," Daphne says, pointing at the far end of the showroom. "By the window."

The damn thing is made of cement and has to weigh a hundred pounds.

"Don't you have a dolly?"

"I can help," she offers, but I wave her away.

"Never mind, I have it."

I muscle it over to the spot she pointed out and then wipe my brow with my forearm. "Why don't you have employees?"

"No need." She shrugs and then taps her lips with a forefinger as if she's contemplating relocating the planter.

"It stays," I say. "It looks great."

"Fine. I don't have employees because they'd just ask a bunch of questions that I don't like answering. And from the experiences I've had, they're not reliable."

"What if you're sick? Or on vacation?"

"Then I close the shop. But I'm rarely sick, and I don't take vacations."

I stare at her as she checks a spreadsheet on her clipboard. "You're kidding me."

"About what?"

"No vacations? What kind of fresh hell is that?"

She just laughs. "I *like* what I do, Jack. I don't need a vacation from it. Besides, where would I go? And with whom? My sisters don't travel. And you know I'm more comfortable surrounded by things I know. I'd hate to sit in an airplane and feel the grief of the person who sat there before me because they were on their way to a funeral. It's best if I stay put."

"You have shields against those things," I remind her.

"Most of the time." She checks something off on her list and then changes the subject. "Okay, now I need to shift these couches. I want to move different ones over here so they can be seen through the front window."

We spend the next hour moving furniture. Watching her work is fascinating.

"How are you protecting yourself right now?" I ask. "How are you not feeling a flood of emotions? You've touched at least a dozen antiques in the past fifteen minutes alone."

"I've learned to reach out with just a thread in my mind. If it's an unfamiliar piece, I send out a little thread to see if there is any malicious intent in it. Nine times out of ten, there isn't, and then I touch it and see its history."

"What about that one time out of ten?"

"I wrap it back up and return it to where it came from."

"Good girl."

She opens a crate, and her eyes dilate for a moment. She must be sending that thread inside to examine the items.

She squeals with glee and pulls out a child's rocking horse.

"Oh, this is just lovely." She caresses the painted wood of the horse's muzzle and along the saddle. "What a fun piece. This was gifted to a little girl in 1933 outside of Atlanta. She loved horses, but her parents couldn't afford a real one, so they gave her this for her birthday. She played on it for years."

Her expression falls.

"But she died when she was nine. Polio. They put the toy up in an attic and the family forgot about it until they cleaned the house out a few months ago to sell."

"And now it can bring another child some joy."

Her smile slips easily back into place, and my heart shifts.

"Oh, I hope so. I sincerely hope so. Let's put it in the window, shall we?"

"Your wish is my command."

I carry the horse to the platform in the window and set it next to an old baby carriage.

"Where did this come from?" I ask, testing out the wheels as I roll it back and forth.

"Idaho," Daphne says. "It's from 1910. It's really too old to use for a baby now, but I thought it would make a great photography prop or something for someone. It once held twins."

"They must have been tiny. This thing isn't big."

"They were tiny," she agrees with a soft smile. "And very loved."

"How do you do this?"

Her eyes meet mine. "How can I not? Everything I've told you is happy."

"But it's all about people who've died."

"Death is a part of life, Jackson. You know that better than anyone. Besides, all of these items brought people immense joy. I want to pass that on to someone else."

I blow out a breath and then shake my head. "Okay. What's next?"

CHAPTER FOUR

"For all of these things, I am not the least bit sorry."
-Carl Panzram

He's been watching his girls through the mirrors in their homes. They thought they could hide from him. That their pathetic spells could keep him away.

It's almost laughable. But they've underestimated him at every turn for as long as he can remember. They have to be punished for that.

Yes. There's no other way. But the punishments will be so sweet. And the girls will appreciate him. *Love* him for showing them where they went wrong.

He's almost embarrassed by their lack of gratitude. His mother would have given him thirty lashes and sent him into the cellar for a week if he'd been even *half* as disrespectful as those girls.

He blames Ruth for that. She needs to be punished, as well.

But for now, he's shifted his focus to Daphne. Ah, his sweet Daphne. She's the gentlest of the three. The softest—with a heart of gold. He's not supposed to have a favorite, but in his heart of hearts, Daphne is the one who brings him the most joy.

He's excited to get started on this phase of the game. Daphne will be so thrilled by his work. So *grateful*.

He's been drifting in spirit form for a long while, and he likes this better than trying to inhabit another stupid mortal. The last one was such a disappointment. This time, he plans to do things another way.

It won't be as satisfying as holding the knife, but he'll make do.

He watches her. Not Daphne, not yet, but another woman with hair the color of fire and big, blue eyes.

A new toy.

She stands in front of the mirror in her bathroom, looking right at him as she pins her hair on the top of her head, getting ready for a bath.

"Oh, aren't you beautiful?" he croons. The toy's eyes glaze over as the trance settles in. "That's right, pin that hair up. You don't want to get it wet in the bath, do you? Such pretty hair."

He wishes he could reach through the mirror and

touch her. Feel that hair in his fingers, the smooth skin. But he's not that strong.

Not yet.

"Take off your clothes now." He watches as the woman steps out of her pants and pulls her sweatshirt over her head. "Oh, yes. You're just lovely with all that white skin. Those pink nipples. Yes, a bath is just the thing, isn't it? Is the water hot enough?"

She moves to the side of the tub and tests the temperature, then turns off the tap since the tub is almost full.

"Ah, ah, ah. Don't forget the blow-dryer. That's it." She plugs the blow-dryer into the outlet, and he smiles with delight when she steps into the tub, sits, and electrocutes herself to death.

CHAPTER FIVE

Daphne

"I have an idea," Jack says after I turn the lock in Reflections' door after a long day of rearranging my merchandise and waiting on customers.

"What's that?" I ask.

"I don't know if you heard, but I sold my parents' house a few years back."

"I heard," I confirm and remember how my stomach had twisted at the news. I'd spent many hours in that house with Jack's parents. I'd loved them very much.

"Well, I kept all of the furniture. Especially the *antiques* that my mama collected over the years."

I feel my eyes light in interest. "Did you keep that gorgeous folding writing desk she had in the corner of the living room?"

"I kept everything," he confirms, and my heart gives a little leap. "It's all in a garage on Oliver's property. Would you be interested in any of it for the shop?"

I nod and know exactly where I would put that desk.

In my living room.

"Absolutely. I could consign it for you here. Or even buy the pieces outright from you to sell. Either way."

"Let's go look at it," he suggests.

"Now?"

He nods and tucks his hands into his pockets. "No time like the present."

I could use the distraction, and I remember that Jack's mom had some beautiful pieces. "I'd love to see it."

"Let's go, then."

I gather my purse, make sure everything is locked up tight, and the next thing I know, I'm in the front seat of Jack's car, headed out of the city.

Oliver doesn't live as far out as the bayou, but he's on the edge of the city where there's more space—where the homes are spread out a bit. He's owned his property for many years. At least, for as long as I can remember.

When Jack pulls into Oliver's driveway, nostalgia hits me. We used to come here for dinner every Sunday afternoon—mudbugs or a fish fry. It was the best food. And some of the best company.

When Jack turned his back on me all those years ago, I didn't just lose him. I lost his family, too. Oliver, and his wife, Annabelle, who were always nothing but wonderful to me.

Jack reaches over and squeezes my hand, catching my attention.

"You okay?" he asks, his voice soft.

"Of course." He comes to a stop. I get out of the car and stretch my back. "Which garage is the stuff in?"

"Over there," he says as he points to the smaller of the two buildings on the property. "The other one is Oliver's shop."

"Is he still making all of that beautiful furniture?"

"Woodworking is in his blood," Jack says. "He'll never stop."

"I still have the little step stool he made me. I love it."

Jack unlocks a big garage door and lets it slide up. As light filters inside, I see that almost everything is covered or wrapped in tarps, which is absolutely perfect.

"It's going to be like unwrapping Christmas gifts," I say with a grin as we step inside. "There are no snakes in here, right?"

"No snakes, no critters," Jack confirms. "It's a safe place. Let's start uncovering this stuff."

We start on the left, intending to make a circle around the garage, and I'm giddy at what we'll find. When Jackson uncovers a gorgeous dresser, I sigh.

"Your mama had such good taste." I run my hand over the dark chestnut and am immediately back in Jack's parents' bedroom, watching as they dance around the room, laughing. It makes my heart happy. "Oh, this is fun."

"What is it?" he asks.

"They had so much fun together." I shrug a shoulder. "I could definitely sell this piece for you. I have a buyer in mind already."

"Great. Let's keep going. Otherwise, we'll be here until tomorrow morning," he suggests. We make our way through half a dozen pieces, all gorgeous and in excellent shape, when we hear footsteps approaching the building.

"Well, hello there," Oliver says as he pokes his head inside. "Thought I heard someone out here. Figured it was you, though I didn't expect both of you. Glad it ain't thieves."

I laugh and hurry over to kiss Oliver's cheek. "Not this time. How are you, Ollie?"

"I get by just fine, Miss Daphne."

But I step back and frown when I look up at the handsome man. His eyes are a bit sunken and shadowed, the circles darker than I've ever seen them.

"Are you sure you're feeling okay?" I ask him.

"Don't you worry about me," he says. "I have a wife that does enough of that."

"How is Miss Annabelle?"

"Fit as a fiddle and as beautiful as ever. She said to let you know she has some gumbo on the fire and that you should stay for it."

"I won't argue with gumbo," I say and pat his arm.

"We're just going through some of Jack's parents' antiques."

"I think it's time to sell some things," Jack adds.

"There are some fine pieces in here," Oliver says with a nod. "Should make someone happy. Y'all come in any time. The food'll be nice and hot for you."

"Thank you," I call after him and then turn to Jack. "Is he really okay?"

"I see it, too," Jackson replies with a sigh. "He's been acting pretty normal, but he just looks...beat. I'll mention it to Annabelle. I'm sure she'll make him go to the doctor."

"Good. I think he needs to." I pull a tarp and grin in happiness when I uncover the writing desk. "Here it is."

"Mom loved that thing," Jack says. "I don't know where she got it."

"I'll tell you." I run my hand over the top of the piece and smile softly. "Oh, it's older than I thought. 1818. This was built in Maryland. Came here with a young couple who wanted to make a life in New Orleans. That family passed it down to your mama."

"I didn't know my mother's family," Jack admits and shoves his hands into his pockets.

"She was the last of them," I reply softly. "Look, Jack, I was going to offer to buy this from you for my personal collection, but you should keep it in your family. Pass it on to someone someday."

"You don't need to buy it," he says. "It's yours, Daph."

I shake my head. But, oh, how I long to own this piece. It's pulled at me since the first time I saw it.

"If you *ever* want it back, you only have to say the word."

His smile is quick. "So noted. Let's get through some more of this before we go in for dinner."

"My stomach is growling," I say as I pull back a tarp and gasp.

The piano.

"I'm so sorry, Mr. Jimmy." I'm at the stove, cooking up some soup for the man sitting at the table, his head in his hands. Jack's at work, and I don't want Jimmy to be alone.

His wife died only a week ago.

I set a bowl of soup on the table at his elbow, and he catches my hand before I can move away.

"You see things, Daphne."

"Yes, sir."

"Will you look? For me? Maybe it'll give me a moment with her, I just need something."

Goddess, I hurt for him. Jimmy and Elaine were so in love. So wonderful together.

Her death almost destroyed him.

"Sure. What should I touch?"

He looks around the room, almost desperately, and then points at the piano in the corner. "She loved to play. It was her favorite part of the day."

"Then I'll start there."

I take a deep breath, sit on the bench, uncover the keys, and then rest my fingers on the ivories and smile. "Oh, Jimmy. You're right. Playing was the best part of her day."

"Can you talk to her? Can you tell her that I love her?"

His voice is full of tears.

"No, you know that's not my gift. I can only see what *was*. But she did love this piano. More than that, she loved you and Jackson. Being a wife and mother filled her cup, Mr. Jimmy."

"I know." *He drops back into his chair and wipes his eyes.* "I know it did."

"She was playing that morning." *I frown as the image comes into my head, sharp as can be.* "She was playing and smiling. Fiddling with a new song. Something for your anniversary. Then, she felt so tired. Just so, so tired, and thought she'd take a nap before she got dinner started.

"She went up to the bedroom and laid down, thinking of you and Jack. Wondered if maybe Jack would come for dinner, too. And she could make some strawberry shortcake for dessert. She wanted to have both of her men under one roof for a meal. She missed Jack after he moved out and started taking classes in the city. But she was so proud of him, too. And so happy that he was with a nice girl.

"And then, she just drifted off to sleep. No dreams. No pain. Just...sleep."

I shake myself out of the vision and whip my head around to stare at Mr. Jimmy, who's sobbing quietly now and watching me with so much grief and guilt, I feel ashamed for saying everything I just did.

"I'm sorry. I shouldn't have said all of that."

"No, you should." *He swallows and wipes at the tears on his cheeks.* "Now I know what her last moments were like. Damn it, Daphne, it was my fault."

"No—"

"Yes. I'm the one who didn't fix that gas leak correctly. Didn't want to spend a few hundred dollars to hire someone to handle it the right way. And because of that, because of a few dollars, my baby's gone."

I don't know what to do. What to say.

"Daph?"

I blink and glance over at Jack, who's watching me with a scowl. "Huh?"

"Where'd you go, sweets?"

"Oh. Just memories. You can definitely sell the piano. Let's move on."

"Daph—"

"Let's move on," I say again and uncover another piece.

After thirty minutes, we've mentally cataloged everything in the garage. He has a small fortune just sitting here.

"I'm happy to consign all of this for you, Jack."

"Awesome, thank you. I'll make arrangements for it to be shipped to Reflections."

I nod as he closes the door, locks it, and then turns to me. "Let's grab some gumbo."

"Let's talk first."

"No." I rest my hand on his shoulder. I can't read his thoughts like I once could, and that's for the best. "I'm hungry, and Miss Annabelle went to a lot of trouble. So, we'll go eat."

He curses under his breath but doesn't argue as I set off for the house.

———————

"Miss Annabelle hasn't changed a bit." I lean back against the car seat with the window rolled down, enjoying the hot air as it blows through my hair. "She's sweet and sassy all at once. And makes the best gumbo ever—don't tell Millie I said that."

He laughs and nods, turning onto my street. "She's the best. Mind if I come up for a bit?"

"We've spent a *lot* of time together today," I point out.

"Sick of me?"

Surprisingly, no. I'm not sick of him at all.

"Not yet."

He laughs and cuts the engine, smiling over at me. "Please, can I come up with you?"

"You're such a pouter." I roll my eyes but don't tell him no as we get out of the car and head to my front door. "Fresh blood on my door. Millie's been here."

"I'm not new to any of these things, yet that gives me the willies," Jackson confesses as I unlock the door and step inside.

"Yeah, well, it makes her feel better." I kick off my

shoes and pad into the kitchen for a glass of wine. "Want some?"

"Nah, I'm good."

He waits while I pour.

"Okay, what is it?" I ask when I return to the living room and sit on the couch facing him. "Just say it already."

"What happened in the garage?" he asks. "When you touched the piano, it was different from the other things."

"Just a memory."

"Bullshit."

But his voice is mild as he sits back and watches me.

"Okay, we're being open and honest, right? Because of this predicament we're in?"

He raises a brow. "That's a mild term, but yes."

"I don't want to tell you." There, I said it. "I don't want to talk about it with you, Jackson. Because I don't trust that you'll hear me and not freak out. Because the last time I tried to talk to you about something important I saw, you walked out on me. You left and tore me to pieces."

"I was young," he says and stands, pushing his hand through his hair. "Jesus, Daph, I was *so* young. And hurt. Grieving. Sad. And I wanted to be angry. You were the closest target."

"Age has nothing to do with treating someone with respect." I stand as well and cross my arms over my chest. "You wouldn't listen to me. I told you what I saw because you *needed* to know. And it nearly killed me. I almost didn't tell you."

"For a long time, I wished you hadn't," he says and holds his hands out at his sides. "I didn't want to know that my dad killed himself. I couldn't deal with it. And, yes, I was horrible that day, but since we're being honest here, I was horrible for a long time. Going into the Army and leaving was the best thing for me. Because I was an asshole. And so damn angry."

"I can't risk you leaving again." I shrug when his eyes narrow. "We need you to help finish this thing with *him*, whether I like it or not. And trust me when I say, I don't like it. I didn't want you to be the sixth. I didn't want us to need you."

"I'm flattered." His voice is dry as he crosses his arms over his chest.

"But you are the sixth, and we *do* need you. So, I'm not going to tell you anything that I think will send you running for the hills. Not until he's gone, and we're free to live our lives like not-so-normal people."

That makes his lips twitch.

"I won't leave."

His voice is strong. Sure. Free from frustration now and completely calm. His eyes never waver, and he drops his arms from his chest.

"I won't go, Daphne. Just tell me what you saw."

I want to. Goddess, I want to.

"Hey." He crosses to me and frames my face in his hands. The warmth that seeps into me is like a sweet welcome home. I don't think I've felt warm since the day he walked out on me all those years ago. "You can tell me. I won't turn my back on you again."

I take a deep breath, let it out slowly, and with my eyes on his, I tell him what I saw when I touched the piano.

"It was a memory, like I said," I add when I'm finished relaying the story. "And, Jack, it's my fault."

I feel the tears fill my eyes as he drops his hands from my face and takes a step back.

The retreat is a slice through my heart.

"It's my fault that he killed himself," I continue while I can still make the words come. "He felt so guilty, even though he didn't cause her death. It was a horrible mistake. An awful accident. But I told him too much, and he just couldn't handle it. And then, just a few weeks later, he took his own life. I can't tell you what I wouldn't give to be able to go back and do it differently. To shut my damn mouth and not tell him everything I saw that day. It destroyed him, Jack. And it's my fault."

And just like that, my worst fears come to life.

Jack turns his back on me, drops his head, and sighs.

CHAPTER SIX

Jackson

For fuck's sake, how much more will be piled onto me this week? I take a deep breath and blow it out. I don't want Daph to see this grief and hurt.

She doesn't deserve that.

"You're going to go," she whispers behind me, and I turn to find her looking absolutely defeated.

"No." I step back to her and wrap my arms around her, pulling her against me as I rock back and forth, comforting us both. "No, I'm not leaving. I just needed a minute, that's all."

She clings to me in relief, and I pull back to wipe the tears from her gorgeous cheeks.

"You've been carrying a burden that isn't yours," I say gently as she sniffles. She shakes her head, but I continue. "Listen to me very carefully, Daphne. My father *chose* to end his life. He couldn't carry the grief and guilt, and that's on him. I feel awful for him, and I wish he'd gone to someone for help. Oliver. Me. Miss Sophia. But it's not your fault that he took the information you gave him and used it as fuel for his actions. Hell, we don't know for sure that that's what happened."

"Yeah." She winces and sniffs. "We do, Jack."

I sigh and lean in to kiss her forehead. God, she smells good.

"I messed up, sweets," I admit in a low voice. "I messed up really bad, and I regret it more than I can tell you. I'm so sorry that I hurt you. More than that, I'm sorry that I lost your trust."

She swallows hard but doesn't deny it.

"I don't want to start over," I continue softly. "I don't want to do that because it would basically negate everything we had before, and it was damn good before, Daph."

She grins. "We were babies."

"Maybe so, but it was still great. The best thing that ever happened to me. So, I don't want to start over. But I do want to begin again."

"Oh, Jack, I don't think that's a good idea."

"I know that it means you'll have to trust me. And maybe you're not ready for that yet. But I'll earn it. In the meantime, I want to get to know you better. I want to just *be* with you, sweets."

"Every single time you called me that before," she admits softly, "it turned my knees to Jell-O. You always used to give me butterflies."

I step closer, dragging my fingertips up and down her arm. "Is that only in the past tense?"

"I'm not telling you all my secrets, Jackson Pruitt."

I laugh, enjoying everything about her.

"Fair enough. Let me take you out to dinner tomorrow night."

"Like, on a date?"

"Hell, yes. On a date."

She seems to mull it over and then shrugs. "Okay. But I want to wear a fancy dress and heels and drink champagne."

"Expensive date, it is." I laugh when she waggles her eyebrows. "You always did like to dress up."

"I still do. If there was a market for antique clothing, I'd sell it."

"There isn't?"

"Not really. It's a very niche market, so I leave it to others and just focus on furniture."

"I'll pick you up at six. Should I get you here or at the shop?"

"Here," she says with a small smile. "Thanks."

"No, thank *you*." I kiss her forehead again and then make myself back away. "I'd better go. If you need anything, or if *anything* happens, call me."

"Okay."

She walks me to the door and is still watching me drive away when I take off down the street.

Instead of driving back to Oliver's for the night, I

detour to Lucien and Millie's place in the Garden District.

Their house is big and old, and if what they told me the other night is true, they lived in it in a previous life.

Who am I to say it isn't true? I've seen some crazy things in this life.

I climb the stairs and knock on the door, but as soon as my knuckles hit the wood, it opens, and Millie grins at me.

"Did you know I was coming?"

"I'm psychic, remember?" She laughs at my blank look. "Kidding. No, I didn't know you were coming, but I saw your lights when you pulled in. Is Daph with you?"

"No, I just left her. And I don't know what made me come over here, other than I'm restless and want to talk."

"Then come on in." She steps back, and just as I walk inside, Lucien descends their grand staircase. He's in a T-shirt and shorts, his hair a mess, and he pushes his black-rimmed glasses up his nose.

"Hey, Jack."

"Hi."

"Jack's lovesick and wanted to come over to talk about Daphne."

"I, uh..." I scowl and push my hand through my hair. "That's not why I'm here."

Millie laughs and takes my hand, tugging me into a library off the foyer and offering me a seat.

"Holy shit, that's a lot of books."

"A lot," Millie agrees as Lucien pours a snifter of brandy and passes it to me.

"What *do* you want to talk about?" Lucien asks as he sits with a glass of his own. "You didn't come here just to say hello."

"No, I didn't." I lean my elbows on my knees and stare down into the brandy. "I love her."

Millie smiles serenely, and Lucien waits as if there's more to be said.

"That's it."

"Is there a problem?" Lucien asks. "Of course, you love her. She's meant for you."

"Is she? Or is this part of the game?" I look up at both of them, then stand and pace the room. "Am I being manipulated by this piece of shit?"

"Do you honestly think that what you feel for her isn't real?" Millie demands with a scowl. "Good grief, Jack, you've been in love with her for *years*. Why would what's happening now change that?"

"Maybe I'm crazy," I mutter, shaking my head. "And I know I sound like an asshole. I don't mean to. I had a great day with Daphne today, and we cleared the air about a lot of things. I'm even taking her out tomorrow for dinner."

"That's so awesome," Millie says and claps her hands.

"But I want to know that everything I'm feeling, everything that's happening between Daphne and me, is because we're genuinely feeling this way and not because Horace is fucking with us."

"I get it," Lucien says with a nod. "And I can put your mind at ease. If anything, he'd want you apart, not together. You're stronger together. If the six of us are in the same place, it hurts him. So, he's not going to try to make you fall in love with her. He'll do his best to break you apart."

I sigh in relief and sit back down.

"Wow, you were really worried," Millie says.

"Yeah. Because Daphne and I have been through enough crap, you know? If we're going to be together, I don't want anything interfering in that."

"He's going to mess with your head," Lucien warns me. "He loves smoke and mirrors. He'll play with you, and he'll take delight in it. But you know what's true. You know how you feel about each other."

"Yeah. Shit's about to get really crazy, isn't it?"

"Yes." Millie's face sobers with her answer.

Lucien's phone rings.

"It's Cash." He answers, and his green eyes go cold. "Damn. Let's get everyone here. Jack's here already. Yeah, I'll call Daphne."

He hangs up and taps his phone screen.

"Hey, Daph. I need you to come to our house, please. They found her."

"They found her?" I repeat when Lucien hangs up the phone.

"I'll put some tea on," Millie announces and hurries out of the library toward what I assume is the kitchen.

"Before the others get here, I'm going to give you something." Lucien shifts some books around and then selects one and passes it to me.

"This is a spellbook," I say as I flip through the pages.

"It is, yes."

"Working spells isn't my gift."

"I know that, but I want you to take it. You have magic, Jack."

I start to shake my head, but Lucien continues.

"You have magic. You know how to work it. I want you to cast some protection spells around Oliver and Annabelle's house. To keep you all safe. If they'll join you, all the better."

"I'll take it," I reply just as a knock sounds on the door.

Cash and Brielle hurry into the library, followed by Daphne, who stops short when she sees me.

"How'd you get here so fast from Oliver's?"

"I was here when Cash called," I reply. "I came over to chat a bit."

"I want everyone to drink some of this tea," Millie announces, carrying a tray.

"Of course, you do," Daphne says with a sigh. "Can't we have coffee?"

"No, tea is better." Millie passes the cups around.

"Where was she found?" I ask Cash, cutting to the chase.

"In her home." He sips the tea and then scowls at it. "Christ, Mill, does it have to taste like shit?"

"Where did she live?" Daphne asks.

"Baton Rouge," Cash replies. "And as of right now, it's been ruled a suicide. She got in the bathtub and dropped her blow-dryer in with her."

"Oh, Goddess," Millie whispers, shaking her head. "That's awful."

"And it wasn't a suicide," I add.

"We know that," Cash says. "But I can't get the cops in Baton Rouge to listen to me. They think I'm nuts. And I can't blame them. It sounds crazy."

He stands and paces the room.

"Were her eyes missing?" I ask.

"No." Cash turns and shakes his head. "Her eyes are intact."

"He doctored the photo," Brielle says. "Or conjured it out of thin air."

"It's what *he* wants us to see," Lucien says. "It's all about the eyes this time around."

"Why?" I demand.

"Because Daphne has the sight," Millie reminds me. "It's his sick gift to her."

I feel sick to my stomach and rub my hand over my mouth.

"Isn't that lovely?" Daphne's voice is dry and angry. "Sick son of a bitch. Somehow, he made her kill herself."

"That's my take on it, too," Lucien says, nodding.

"This doesn't help us," Brielle says with frustration.

"He never *helps*," Millie reminds her. "He taunts us."

"So, what do we do now?" I ask. "Do we just sit back and wait?"

Lucien's nod is grim. "Unfortunately, yes."

"Well, hell."

I'VE BEEN STUDYING the book that Lucien sent home with me last night and even cast a few spells at Oliver's place. I'm not a powerful witch, but every little bit helps.

Now it's time to set this aside and enjoy the evening with Daphne. I've been thinking about her all day, too, and about what I said last night at Millie and Lucien's. No one is *making* me feel the way I do about her. I love her because I've always loved her. I took one look at her when I was so stupidly young and knew without a doubt that she was it for me.

Nothing this asshole does can change that.

I pull up to Daphne's apartment, knowing that I'm early.

I couldn't wait to see her.

I jog up the steps in my slacks and jacket, and when she opens the door, all irritation leaves her eyes when she sees the flowers in my hands.

"You're early." But there's no censure when she takes the flowers and buries her nose in them.

"I know. I wanted to see you."

"Well, come on in. I'm still putting on my makeup."

I follow her back to her bathroom, and just as I used to do before, I hop onto the countertop and watch her apply her makeup.

"We used to do this all the time," I murmur and lift a tube of mascara, studying it.

"And you'd make me laugh and mess up," she says with a snort. "You big jerk."

"You loved it."

"No way. I wasted a lot of makeup. Do you know how expensive this stuff is?"

I just smile at her in the mirror, and she goes back to brushing something pink onto her cheeks.

"You don't need the makeup. You're gorgeous without it."

"I like it." She sets down the brush and starts on her eyes. "What did you do today?"

"I studied."

That surprises her enough to have her gaze flying to meet mine. "What are you studying?"

"Lucien gave me a book last night." I shrug a shoulder. "How was work today?"

"Good. Great, actually. Some new pieces arrived that I'm in love with, and I finally sold a sofa that I've had for several years. It just needed the right buyer."

She grins, examines her handiwork in the mirror,

and then rushes into the bedroom to change her clothes.

"Stay in there!" she calls out.

"Okay." I fiddle with a brush, listening to her rustling around. And then she comes to the door of the bathroom and does a little turn.

My mouth goes dry.

"Holy crap." I swallow hard and take her in. Her red hair is sleek and wavy, and her blue dress hugs every delectable curve. I hop off the counter. "Come here."

"Did I forget something?"

She wanders into the room. I turn her away from me to face the mirror as I stand behind her and meet her eyes in the glass.

"You are every dream I've ever had." I kiss the ball of her shoulder and slide my hand over her stomach. "Every wish. Jesus, you're all I think about. And when I was overseas, going through hell on Earth, it was the thought of your sweet face that got me through each day."

"Jack." She whispers my name and raises her hand to cup my cheek. "You got really romantic in your old age."

I smile against the tender flesh of her neck.

"I should have said all of this and more years ago. I should have come home and fought for you. Apologized."

"It's happening the way it's meant to." She turns in my arms to face me. "I always hate it when Millie or Miss Sophia says that, but it's true, Jack. This is how our story was meant to go. At least, we made it back around to the good stuff."

I grin and lean in to gently rub my lips over hers. She inhales and pushes her fingers into my hair, holding on as I kiss her slowly, remembering every touch, every sigh.

And just as my hands rise to cup her cheeks, the mirror above the sink falls and shatters into a million pieces.

We jump apart, startled.

"Don't move." I pick her up and walk out of the bathroom. "You're not wearing shoes."

"What the hell was that, Jack?"

"The mirror fell."

She shakes her head. "Things don't just fall like that. Not for no reason."

"Stop." I kiss her cheek. "It just fell, Daph. Now, where's your dustpan and broom?"

CHAPTER SEVEN

"I will have you removed if you don't stop. I have a little system of my own."
-Charles Manson

"**Y**ou little slut," he mutters as he watches his Daphne smile coyly at that piece of shit, Jackson. "Don't you *dare* let him touch you!"

But she can't hear him. No, she just lets Jackson put his filthy hands on her and leans into him. God, it makes Horace sick to his stomach.

If he still had a stomach.

"You ungrateful little bitch," he spits out. He wants to reach through the mirror so badly. To kill that asshole with his own two hands and then punish his girl the way she *needs* to be punished.

The anger is swift and all-consuming, and when Daphne lifts her face for a kiss, he loses all control.

He bangs his fists against the glass in fury. Suddenly, it breaks, and he can't see them anymore.

"Little cunt," he mutters, retreating from Daphne's home and flying up into the sky. "That little *brat*. What is she thinking? I got rid of him once, sent him away, and now he's *back*? Unacceptable."

Breaking the mirror depleted Horace's energy, and he has work to do—so much work to do. More than he originally thought. Obviously, Daphne has lessons to learn.

"She never was the smartest of my girls," he mutters as he finds the house he's been searching for, just on the edge of town. "She needs more detail. More attention. She *needs* me. But that's what I'm here for."

He nods in satisfaction and takes his place behind the mirror, delighted when he doesn't have to wait long.

He has the most satisfying energy source. It was too easy. Too perfect, really.

As the man stands before the mirror, washing his hands, Horace grins gleefully. And when he raises his head, Horace begins the spell and pulls energy from the host in a steady stream that makes him feel energized and full of adrenaline.

He's careful not to take too much—not to take it all. He doesn't want to kill this one, not yet. The time isn't right.

The man slumps forward, and Horace flies up, refreshed and ready for his next toy.

He has the perfect one in mind.

The trip north doesn't take long, and when he moves behind the mirror, he smiles. Yes, everything's working out just right.

"There you are. Did you have a bad day?"

The woman on the other side of the glass scowls at her phone, muttering under her breath. She's only wearing a bra and underwear. She's fat, much too big for his tastes, and he's grateful that he doesn't have to touch her. He'd give her more pain, punish her for her gluttony.

It *is* a sin.

Maybe he wishes he could touch her, after all. Show her how stupid she is.

But perhaps there's a way.

She glances up into the mirror, and her brown eyes cloud over when he begins speaking to her.

"You forgot your knife," he croons, feeling much calmer now that he's focused on his work. "You'd best go fetch it."

Without a word, the toy leaves the bathroom and returns with a big kitchen blade—a chef's knife.

"Is it sharp?" he asks. He misses the weight of a knife in his hands. The way it feels when it slices through flesh. "You'd best test it."

Horace's breath catches when the toy glides the blade up her arm, cutting from wrist to elbow.

She cries out.

He sighs in delight.

"Oh, yes. Yes, this is perfect. Now, let's trim some of that fat off you, shall we?"

CHAPTER EIGHT

Daphne

I shove my feet into my slippers and rush back into the bathroom. I'll be damned if Jack will clean up the glass by himself.

"Jack, things don't just randomly fall off walls," I insist when I hurry in and see that he's already sweeping up pieces of glass. Damn it. I really loved this mirror. "There's always a reason. A ghost. A poltergeist."

"Faulty nails," he adds and points to the little nail sticking out of the wall. "That thing wasn't sturdy enough to hold this."

"It's been hanging there for years," I inform him. "I've never had a problem before. Oh, Goddess, what if it's Hor—*him?*"

"There's a damn strong protection spell on your place," he reminds me. "There's no way he got in here and broke this thing."

I lean over, touch the frame, and gasp.

Hate.

Fury.

Fire.

"Daph?"

"Jesus." I jump back and scowl at the frame. "That thing is full of awful feelings. And let me just say, it wasn't like that before. It belonged to a woman in Shreveport who loved cats. She was sweet and harmless."

"When did she die?"

I feel my lips twitch. "1988. And that doesn't have anything to do with it. I'm telling you, there was nothing bad in that mirror before."

"I got this," he says and carries the frame, along with a bag of broken glass, out the door to the trash.

When he returns, he frowns.

"What are you doing?"

"I don't feel like going out now." I unfasten my earrings, but before I can take off the necklace, Jack crosses to me and frames my face.

"Hey, it's just a mirror. It fell. We're still going out for dinner. You deserve it. Besides, we have reservations."

"Where?" I ask and play with one of the buttons on his shirt, enjoying the way he feels when he stands so close to me.

"Café Amelie."

I narrow my eyes. "How did you know that's my favorite restaurant?"

"I'm never going to give up my sources," he says with a confident grin.

"On the way back, can we swing by the shop so we can pick up another mirror? I have just the one I want in mind."

"Sure. I'll even hang it for you. With a better nail. I promise it won't fall."

I change into my heels and refasten my earrings. I won't tell him again that I don't think that mirror just *fell*. I don't know what it could have been, but things don't just randomly fall.

Maybe Millie would know, if she came over. I don't like the idea of asking her to drop her shields, though. Her psychic gifts are so strong, so powerful, they could hurt her. Keeping those shields in place is the best protection for her.

No one was hurt. The mirror is gone. End of story.

Jackson leads me to his car.

"Oh, and by the way, I don't kiss on the first date." Which is a silly thing to say because he's already kissed me.

But still. It's the principle.

Jack laughs and swings out into traffic. "I remember."

"THE MIRRORS ARE OVER HERE," I say as we walk into the shop. I flip on some lights, and my heels clip on the old hardwood floor. "I have the perfect one in mind. I wanted to buy it as soon as it arrived, but I didn't have anywhere to put it."

"But now you do," Jack adds with a smile.

"Now, I do."

Dinner was *easy*. That's the best way to describe it. There was no weirdness—nothing uncomfortable at all. We had plenty of delicious food and a little wine. Our conversation was light. I didn't want to dig into the past or ask a bunch of questions when we were sitting in the middle of a restaurant full of people.

"Have I mentioned that you look amazing?" he asks as he slips up behind me and rubs my shoulders.

I'm shocked that I don't purr like a kitten.

"You said something a time or two. Now, focus. Mirror."

"Which one do you want?" he asks but doesn't stop kneading my shoulders.

"That one." I point to an oval mirror with a gold frame.

"Are you sure you don't want that black one?" he asks and points to a mirror below the one I have my heart set on.

"I definitely don't want the black one."

"Why not?"

"A man in New York owned it," I explain and turn to watch his face as I tell him the story. "He was in the mob."

Jack's eyebrow lifts. "Really? Like, the *real* mob?"

"Yeah."

I think back to the first time I touched that mirror and the little jolt it gave me. I didn't expect that.

"I thought you said you send bad juju things back."

"Oh, I do. It's not that this one has bad *juju,* as you put it. In fact, the guy was a lover, not a fighter. And let me tell you, when I say lover, I mean *lover.* The man had more sex than that basketball guy who slept with like twenty thousand women."

"Wilt Chamberlain?"

"Yeah, that guy. I'm not one to judge, but he had *too* much sex. And I don't want that in my house. Now, this oval mirror." I point to the one I want to take home.

"Let me guess. Another little old lady?"

"No." I laugh and shake my head. "It belonged to a nurse, actually. She was tired, overworked, underpaid, and struggling. Single mom. But she was also fierce and determined. And happy. So, I want it. Plus, the gold matches my shower curtain."

Jack laughs as he lifts the mirror off the wall.

"What's so funny?"

"Only you would choose a mirror because it matches your shower curtain."

"I like that shower curtain, thank you very much."

Just as we step back, I catch something move in one of the other mirrors.

"What was that?"

I spin, frantically looking around, but there's nothing there.

"What's wrong?" he asks.

"I swear I thought I saw something move in the reflection."

I turn back to him and see my father standing behind me in the mirror. The smile on his face immediately makes me physically sick.

"Oh, shit."

"Daph?"

"Oh, fuck, Jack."

"Talk to me, baby."

I can't take my eyes off my dad and that horrible smile.

"What do you see, Daphne?"

"My father," I whisper and feel my hands start to shake. "He's standing over my left shoulder."

"Look at me."

I shake my head slowly.

"Damn it, Daphne, look at me. Right now."

My eyes find his, and I feel a little better.

"Your father isn't here, sweets. It's not possible. I promise you."

I return my attention to the mirror and see nothing behind me. It's only the contents of my shop. "I want to go home."

"Let's go."

Jack loads the mirror into the back of his car, and once I shut off the lights and lock the back door, we head out once more toward my apartment.

It's a nice evening. Not too hot. I roll the window

down and enjoy the way the breeze feels. I don't even care if it messes up my hair. It feels too good.

Before long, Jack pulls up in front of my place and carries the mirror up behind me.

"While you hang that, I'm going to change and pour some wine," I inform him. After what happened earlier, I need the entire bottle.

Maybe two.

"Good idea. This won't take long."

He hurries back to his car and returns with a hammer and a handful of nails.

"Why did you have those in your car?"

He licks his lips. "Because I saw this happen, and I wanted to be prepared."

I blink at him and then shift my feet. "When did you see it?"

"A few days ago, I guess." He walks to the bathroom, and I make my way into the bedroom to change my clothes. I love dressing up. But almost as much as that, I adore how it feels to take off the fancy clothes. My leggings and loose sweatshirt feel nice.

I pad barefoot into the kitchen and pour two glasses of red, just as Jack calls out, "Come check it out."

"Oh, I love it." I pass Jackson a glass of wine and smile as I study the mirror. "Dare I say I like it more than the other one?"

"I do, too, actually."

"Thanks for hanging it."

"You're welcome."

"Wanna sit for a while?"

His eyes darken, and he sips his wine. "Yes. I do."

I lead him to the couch and sit on one end, curling my legs under me as I turn to face him where he sits on the other end of the sofa.

"Should we talk about what happened before?" Jack asks.

"No." I shake my head and block what happened at the shop out of my mind.

"When you're ready, then."

"Where did you go?" I ask, digging into some of the nitty-gritty of our time apart. "After you left New Orleans. I mean, I know you went into the military, but where?"

He talks for a long time about boot camp, traveling, being stationed on the east coast, and then deployed in the Middle East.

"You've done a lot in the years since I saw you last," I say and pour us each another glass of wine. "And all I've done is stay here."

He took his jacket off a while ago, and his shirt-sleeves are rolled up on his forearms. Jackson is tanned and muscled, and his dark hair is just a little too long. It makes him look...*hot*.

"Stop it. You've done a hell of a lot more than that. You started a business—a successful one at that. And you've been dealing with a lot in the past year or so."

"It hasn't been boring," I admit. "I didn't wonder

about where you were back then. I told myself I didn't care."

"I wondered about you every day," he replies, surprising me. "I regretted everything that happened. How I handled it. But I was also so damn angry. I'd think about you. Wonder how you were and what you were doing. But then a crazy fury would wash over me, and I'd block it out. Focus on the job. And then the job consumed everything. I guess being in a warzone does that to you."

My heart aches every time I think of him being in danger.

"I had the premonitions," he continues. "And I knew when my guys were going to die. It was its own kind of torture, Daph. I tried to tell a few of them, but they looked at me like I was fucking crazy."

"I know how that is."

"Yeah." He rubs his hand over his mouth, and I scoot closer to take his other hand. "Yeah, you'd know. So, I stopped telling them. But I also had to block the premonitions because they were driving me insane. With Miss Sophia's help, I finally did."

"You got medals of honor." I smile at his surprised glance. "I kept track of things, even if I did it begrudgingly. You saved lives."

"Not all of them."

"You're only one man, Jack. And as awesome as you are, you can't control everything."

"So, you're saying I'm awesome?"

I laugh and sip my wine.

"How long are you staying here?" I ask, changing the subject.

"Indefinitely."

My eyes find his.

"You're surprised?" he asks.

"Yeah. I thought for sure you'd leave again."

"I did, too, to tell you the truth. I even had a job lined up in Idaho. But I just couldn't go. This is home, Daph. I have people here. And you're here."

He reaches for my hand once more, and I want to pinch myself. Is this real?

"You know, back to the whole telling-each-other-the-truth thing. I'm afraid if we start something between us, and I see something and tell you about it, you'll get angry and leave again. That's why I acted like a big jerk to you since you started coming around again."

"I get it." He sighs and squeezes my hand. "I'm older and wiser now—and no less handsome, of course."

I grin.

"I don't carry around that horrible anger anymore, Daph. It was a disease, eating at me. I got some therapy. The thing is, that wasn't me. That rage isn't who I am. It never has been."

"You were always so laid back and easygoing when we dated before."

"I guess it's true what they say. You never know how

a person will handle grief. I guess I know how *I* handle it."

"I suppose so," I agree quietly. "Thanks for dinner tonight."

"Are you kicking me out?"

I laugh and shake my head. "Not exactly. But I do have to open the shop tomorrow, and we both know that I'm not exactly a morning person."

"You like to ease into the day," he agrees. "I want to talk to you about something I've been thinking about."

"Okay."

"Remember when Millie mentioned that everyone needs to stay together until this is finished? For safety?"

"I remember."

"Well, I know you don't want to do that. And I get it. But I'd like to move in here with you. I'll sleep on the couch. Mind my manners. I don't like the idea of you being here alone."

"Jack, I appreciate the sentiment. I really do. But I don't think it's necessary. I'm perfectly capable of taking care of myself. And like you and everyone else keeps reminding me, I'm safe inside. He can't come in."

"But he can get to you outside."

"So, what? You're just going to follow me around? That seems silly."

"Not silly," Jackson replies, shaking his head. "Your safety is the most important thing. And I know you're an independent woman—and I love that about you—

but damn it, Daphne, I need you to be safe and whole. I don't trust this asshole."

"Well, that's something we can agree on. None of us trusts him. Because, you know, he's a murderous psycho bastard who's obsessed with us and all."

He narrows his eyes on me. "I should stay."

"No, thanks."

Suddenly, I feel sick to my stomach. The way I did the other day when I found the photo on my stoop.

"Oh, Goddess."

"What? What is it?"

I hurry from the couch to the front door and open it. Sure enough, there's another envelope on the mat.

"Fuck," Jack mutters. "How did you know it was here?"

"I get nauseous. And I just...*know*."

We stare down at it.

"I don't want to pick it up," I admit and swallow hard.

Jackson retrieves the envelope, then pulls me back inside and shuts the door.

"The fucker is probably watching," he mutters. We stand, staring down at the envelope. "Why does it feel like it has a heartbeat?"

"More creep factor?" I ask.

"As if he needs more," Jack says. "Do you want me to open it?"

"Yeah. No sense in getting more prints on it. I don't want Cash to yell at me again."

He breaks the seal—a wax one this time—and pulls out another image.

Black and white.

A different woman with short hair. Round cheeks. Many piercings in each ear, two in her nose, and one in her lip.

And, like the other, no eyes.

"I know it's coming by now, that the person won't have eyes, and yet it's alarming. Every single time," I mutter.

"I think it should probably be alarming," he says, his mouth set in a grim line. "The timestamp."

"Two hours ago." I sigh and shake my head. "She's already gone. We have to call the others."

He kisses my head. "Let's just get in the car and go to Millie's. I want this out of your house."

"Good idea. I'll let them know we're coming and call Brielle."

A short fifteen minutes later, we're all sitting in Millie and Lucien's library with the photo resting on the coffee table between us.

"I don't know why we're all here," I say and lift my hands. "We can't do anything about it. This doesn't give us a clue to anything. It's like when the girls were following Brielle. They were just *there*."

"I mean, this isn't quite as bad," Millie puts in. "At least you don't have dead girls following you around everywhere."

"Thank the goddess for small miracles," I agree and

then turn to Brielle. "Wait, you're not seeing them again, are you?"

"No, I haven't seen anything new," she says.

"Can any of you feel the heartbeat?" Jack asks, and four pairs of eyes turn to him. "On the photo."

"I'm not sure what you mean," Lucien says.

"When we hold it," I answer, "we feel heat. And a heartbeat. It's unnerving."

"Fascinating," Lucien says. "I think it's time for a meeting at Miss Sophia's. We need her help and insight on some things."

"If she'll give us the information," Jackson adds. "Every time I ask her for information, she tells me she can't give it to me."

"She can say some things," Millie says. "I think a meeting is a good idea."

"We have to get Mama tomorrow," Brielle reminds us all, and I feel new nerves set up shop in my belly. "She's being released from the hospital, and we're taking her to Miss Sophia's. Maybe we can meet with her then."

"Do we want to do this in front of Mama?" I ask.

"She knows what's going on," Millie says. "She was there on Halloween. I think she can handle it."

"Just let us know what time, and we'll be there," Cash says. "I'll take this photo and add it to the other. And I'll keep my eyes peeled. Daph, would it be possible for you to know what's going on if you touch one of the bodies?"

I want to scream that it won't work. But I touched a body before when it was Brielle's turn, and it was helpful to the investigation.

"Maybe." I shift in my seat. "I can try, if you think it'll help."

"Let's talk to Miss Sophia first," Lucien suggests. "And we'll go from there."

When we're in Jack's car, headed back to my apartment, I reach over to take his hand.

"I don't want to be alone," I admit softly. "I'm scared, Jack."

"Then you won't be alone."

He parks the car, but rather than get out with me, his eyes narrow, and his hands tighten on the wheel.

He's having a vision.

CHAPTER NINE

Jackson

Darkness. Complete darkness surrounds us. I know that all six of us are together, but I can't hear or see the others.

Daphne's hand was just in mine, and now I can't feel her.

I'm here.

Her voice in my head. She's here.

He's trying to fuck with us. Playing games and trying to frighten us.

I'm done being afraid of this son of a bitch.

"Stop playing games and fight like a man!" I yell into the blackness. "You're weak! You're nothing!"

Suddenly, there's an explosion of light, and spirits surround us. Souls. My father, the men who died next to me on the battlefield.

Though isn't that where we are now? A battlefield?

But there are also sinister spirits. The shadows that Brielle saw, the girls' father—they all surround us.

We're in for the fight of our lives.

"Jack?"

I blink and look to my right where Daphne is, frowning with lines of concern creasing her brow.

"What was it?" she asks.

It was how this all ends.

"Let's get inside," I reply and usher Daph up the stairs to her apartment.

"Geez, Jack, you look like you've seen a ghost."

"That would have been less scary," I admit and pace her living room. I tell her about the vision. It only takes a few minutes, yet it felt like I was in it for hours. "It has to be what's meant to happen to make all of this end."

"Or the possible ending," she agrees, nodding. "I think it's good that we're going to Miss Sophia's tomorrow—all of us together. I want you to work on reinforcing your shields, too."

I frown, but she takes my hand and presses it to her cheek.

"I know that this will take a mental toll on you. It's meant to. If you're emotionally and mentally exhausted, you won't be able to fight him off as well."

"I hadn't thought of that." I brush my thumb over the apple of her cheek. Her big blue eyes are somber and full of worry. "But that makes total sense. I'll reinforce the shields."

"Thank you."

She leans into me and rests her head against my

chest the way she used to. God, I want her. Not just physically, although God knows I want her naked and writhing beneath me, too.

But I just want *her*—for the rest of my life. Whether that's eighty more years or three months.

She's meant for me.

"You don't have any of your things," she says and looks up at me. "If you want to go back to Oliver's tonight and come stay tomorrow, I totally understand."

"No." I kiss her head and then pick her up and sit with her in my lap. "I'm not leaving you. I'll stop by Oliver's tomorrow on the way to Miss Sophia's. It won't be the first time I've worn the same clothes two days in a row."

She grins and pushes her fingers through my hair. "Good thing I have a washer and dryer, huh?"

"Handy," I agree.

She leans in to brush her lips across mine, but just as our skin touches, the lights in the apartment go crazy, blinking and flashing around us.

I pull her to me and start to recite the simple banishing spell that Lucien marked in the book he gave me.

"Ashes to ashes, spirit to spirit, take this soul, banish this evil." After the second time through, Daphne joins me. We clasp hands, our voices growing stronger and louder. And then, with a swoosh of wind, the lights calm, and everything goes back to the way it was before.

"He's not supposed to be in here," Daphne says with a shaky voice.

"I'm not convinced he is," I reply.

"Do you think I suddenly have a new ghost?" she asks with an irritated scowl. Only my girl would find a ghost irritating, rather than terrifying.

"I think that the two of us together is powerful magic, Daph. I also think some bad energies are trying to work against us right now. They don't want us together. What they fail to realize is that the more they try to scare us and separate us, the closer to you I'll stick."

She presses her cheek to mine. I've never felt anything so sweet.

"I know I said I'd sleep on the couch." I grin when her eyes find mine once more. "But I'm not going to do that."

"No?"

"No." I brush her fiery hair off her cheek and hook it behind her ear. "I'm going to sleep next to you. Don't worry, I'll be a gentleman."

She snorts, and it makes me grin.

"I'm warning you now, I sleep with a light on."

I raise a brow. "Still?"

She nods.

"Doesn't bother me."

"Okay, then."

"I'M surprised it took you so damn long to move in with her," Oliver says the next day. Daphne went with her sisters to pick up Ruth, and I said I'd meet them at Miss Sophia's later after I check in with Oliver and Miss Annabelle.

"And here I thought we were moving quickly."

Oliver laughs and claps his hand on my shoulder. "She needs you. I'm glad you'll be close by."

"We're headed over to Miss Sophia's today. You're welcome to come. I think we'll need all the help we can get, and I trust you implicitly."

"Annabelle and I will be there. She's making some cobbler, and then we'll head that way."

"Is she ever *not* in the kitchen?"

Oliver laughs and shakes his head. "She says acts of service are her love language, whatever in the Sam Hill that means."

"Well, I'm not complaining. Her cobbler is my favorite. I'll see you both in a bit then."

I toss my bag into the trunk of the car, wave at the older man, and then set off for Miss Sophia's house in the bayou.

Daphne mentioned to me the other day when we were in her shop that the girls plan to build a cottage for their mama on Miss Sophia's property. I wonder where they're thinking of doing it. I could lend a hand. It would be cute on that little hill, right behind where Miss Sophia's cabin sits.

I pull up and turn off the car. When I walk into the house, I already hear voices coming from the kitchen.

Lucien and Cash are already here, but I hear other voices, as well.

"There you are," Miss Sophia says with a welcoming smile. She cups my face in her hands and looks deeply into my eyes. "Blessed be, Jackson."

"And to you," I reply before kissing her cheek.

"We haven't seen you in a long, long time," Gwyneth Bergeron, Lucien's mother, says and rushes over to offer me a hug. "It's good to have you home."

"Thank you."

Aiden, Lucien's dad, shakes my hand, and I'm offered tea and cookies before we sit around the giant table in Miss Sophia's dining room.

Her house is small, but I swear it seems to get bigger when people are here to accommodate everyone. And I wouldn't put it past Miss Sophia to have cast just that kind of spell.

Everyone is welcome at her table.

"Oliver and Annabelle are on their way," I inform everyone. "Has anyone heard from the girls?"

"They're on their way, too," Cash says and pops a cookie into his mouth. "Everything went smoothly with Ruth."

"Good." I turn to Miss Sophia, who's sipping her tea. "Are you sure you're okay with having her here with you? After everything that happened?"

"Ruth has been through hell," she says mildly. "And

she came out the other side. None of it was her fault. I'm looking forward to helping her get stronger and keeping an eye on her to make sure she stays safe from that which tries to harm her."

"We're grateful," Lucien says. "We're *all* grateful."

"Oh, it's my pleasure. Ruth's a strong witch, and we'll need her before long. But that's a story for another day."

I blink at her and want to press her for more information. But I know this woman. And because I do, I know she won't say more until she's good and ready.

Oliver and Miss Annabelle arrive to another round of warm welcomes. Annabelle winks at me as she sits next to Miss Sophia.

She's a strong witch in her own right, and I've always had a soft spot for her. If Oliver is a father to me, then Miss Annabelle is a mother, and I'm grateful to both of them.

She has her black hair tucked under a bright orange and yellow scarf that matches her flowy dress. Miss Annabelle loves bright colors and says the dresses keep her cool in this horrible Louisiana heat.

"You have news," Miss Sophia says, watching me.

"Reading my mind?"

Her smile flashes, and she shakes her head. "No need. It's written all over that handsome face of yours."

"Well, you're right. We have news. But we'll tell it when everyone is here so we only have to say it once."

We hear car doors slam outside. Within minutes,

the girls walk in, Brielle rolling a suitcase behind her, as a smiling Ruth holds Millie's hand. Millie favors her mother, with her long, blonde hair and willowy figure.

"Welcome home," Miss Sophia says as she wraps the other woman in a warm hug. "I'm so happy you're here."

"Thank you, my friend." Ruth leans her forehead against Miss Sophia's. "Thank you."

"Come in, everyone," Miss Annabelle says, ushering the women inside. "There's tea and sweets, and lots of love to go 'round."

"I love it here," Daphne says with a sweet sigh as she slips her hand into mine and rests her head on my biceps. "It always feels so...*safe*."

"What a wonderful compliment," Miss Sophia says with a smile. "Come, everyone. Make yourselves comfortable. Let's pour some tea, shall we?"

It's five minutes of organized chaos, filling cups and spooning up cobbler, laughing, and hugs. And then we're all gathered around the table.

"Where do we start?" Daphne wonders aloud.

"From the beginning," Miss Sophia says calmly. "I think, in order to make sure we're all on the same page and understand exactly what we're up against, we need to start at the very beginning and work our way through what we know so far. Brielle, why don't you begin?"

And so, we do. I hear the same stories they told me the other night at Witches Brew, with new, remembered facts thrown in.

Oliver wraps his arm around Miss Annabelle when

she gasps in horror and has to wipe tears from her gorgeous brown eyes.

When the story winds its way to me, I share about the visions I've had, and Daphne and I piece together what we know about what's happened over the last few days.

"Has anything happened to either of you since the lights flickered last night?" Gwyneth asks as she takes notes in her notebook.

"No, ma'am." I turn to Daphne for confirmation, and she nods silently.

"Well, we've been a busy bunch, haven't we?" Miss Sophia sighs and pours a fresh cup of tea.

How the kettle stays full when we've all poured out of it is a trick I'll have to learn another time.

"Wait." All eyes turn to Daphne, who licks her lips and fidgets with her teacup. "Something else has been happening with me. I didn't tell the others because I didn't want to scare them, but maybe it's tied to this."

"Daphne," Brielle whispers in surprise.

Daph cringes, bites her lip, and then squares her shoulders.

"I've been dreaming about...well, about Daddy."

It's as though the air is sucked right out of the room.

"No," Millie says and closes her eyes. "Oh, Daphne."

"He was gone for so many years," Daphne continues. "The spell we worked with Miss Sophia sent him away, and I didn't dream about him for a long, long time. With all of the manipulation and scare tactics that Hor

—*he* has used this past year, I'm not convinced that it's actually Dad in my dreams now, or if it's merely an illusion meant to mess with me."

"Either way, it's fucked up," Brielle says, anger hard in her voice.

"Agreed," Millie jumps in.

"It could be both," Miss Sophia says, speaking slowly as she thinks it over. "I can rework the spells I cast before. Strengthen them. But, Daphne, part of this will be up to you."

Daphne leans in, listening. "In what way?"

"You have to stand up to him. I know he frightened you when you were children, but you're not a weak child anymore. You have tools, and you have grit. You don't need anyone's permission to stand up to him and tell him that he's not welcome in your head. He has no control over you. No power when it comes to you."

Daphne blinks rapidly. "Why didn't I think of that? It's always been an immediate reaction to be afraid."

"Because when you see him, you're that little girl again," Miss Annabelle adds. "And that's normal, if you ask me. But Miss Sophia is right, child. You need to stand up to that bully and tell him to get the hell out of your head."

Daphne takes a deep breath. "Just the thought of it makes my hands sweat, but you're right. Except, what if he *does* have power? What if he can still hurt me?"

"I think *scaring* you was always his primary goal,"

Aiden says, jumping in for the first time. "You said that he'd laugh or smile?"

"Yes."

"Then the fear is what drives him. Show him that you're not afraid of him."

Daphne laughs shakily as Cash's phone rings. He stands to take the call in the kitchen. "Even if I *am* afraid of him."

"You're standing up to a bully," I remind her. "Dead or alive, he's still a bully. Tell him off. You'll feel better."

She nods. "Okay. I'll do it."

Cash walks back into the room, his expression grim.

"What is it?" Brielle asks her husband.

"They found the second victim," Cash says with a sigh and pulls his laptop out of his bag. "She was in Shreveport. A buddy of mine from that PD is sending me images from the scene."

He punches some keys and then rubs his hand over his mouth as he examines the screen.

"I'm not showing this to you," he says and closes the laptop.

"Did she electrocute herself like the first?" Millie asks.

"No." He swears under his breath. "God, I feel sick."

"Take a deep breath," Miss Sophia suggests. "What did he do to her?"

Ruth offers Cash a glass of water. He takes it and drinks deeply. "He cut her up. Cut her up really bad."

I scowl. "So he's back to doing things himself then?"

"No," Cash says, shaking his head. "There were no other prints, no signs of another person being there at all."

"Maybe he cleaned up after himself," I suggest, but Cash is already shaking his head.

"There was so much damn blood. There's no way another person was in that room," he says, his voice growing harder with anger. "She cut herself up."

"This is insane," I mutter and have to stand to pace the room. "How is he doing this? How can he *make* these people kill themselves?"

"Through mirrors?" Oliver asks, surprising us all because he's usually content to listen and watch. "Could he manipulate them through mirrors? I want to say I've read something about that before."

"He could be using them as a window or portal," Miss Sophia says, speaking slowly as she thinks it over. "It could be how he's traveling, as well. It's so unusual. So *odd*. I'll have to do some research."

"Does anyone know if Horace was a scrying master?" Millie asks.

"Do you know?" Daphne asks her mother, whose eyes grow round with confusion.

"Me? I don't even know the man."

Daphne and her sisters scowl in confusion, but Miss Sophia shakes her head, signaling for them not to jump in with questions.

"Ruth, you remember Horace. He worked at your home when the girls were little. A handyman."

"I know that he's the man we're working to defeat and that he's trying to hurt my girls, but I don't remember knowing him at all. If he worked at the house, I didn't hire him."

"You have no memory of him hanging around the house?" Brielle asks with a small frown.

"She was already being tormented by then," Miss Sophia says with a sigh. "Oh, Ruth. I'm so sorry."

"Well, whether I know him or not, we're going to kick his sorry ass straight to hell, I'll tell you that right now," Ruth says, straightening her spine. "Because like Daphne, I'm sick of being afraid. And I'm done being used. This will *end*."

"Attagirl," Miss Annabelle says and pats Ruth's hand. "You're absolutely right. He's had his fill of fun or whatever it is he's doing. It's time for this to end. For all your sakes."

"How?" I wonder aloud. "How do we end it? That's the one question I've been asking since I became involved. The one that no one will answer."

"Wait." Brielle holds up a hand. "The day we defeated him at his house, when we were able to save Mama, that was during a full moon. And then when we defeated him again in the field, it was the full hunter's moon, on Halloween, when the veil was the thinnest."

"Please don't tell me we have to wait for Halloween again," I say, shaking my head. "That's too damn far away."

"No, but there's a lunar eclipse coming," Millie says,

standing with excitement. "And that's only two weeks away. A full moon eclipse is *very* powerful and may be exactly the thing we need."

"I love this idea," Daphne says with a nod. "Miss Sophia?"

The older woman simply smiles. "I think that's a good idea."

CHAPTER TEN

"I certainly wanted for my mother a nice, quiet, easy death like everyone else wants."
-Edmund Kemper, The Co-Ed Killer

Despite taking the energies from his toys, along with the *perfect* toy, he felt depleted after the six of them spent time together.

It brought him to his knees and made him small. It must be what's making him hurt the way he does now.

It had been so much easier, so much better before when he was still alive and only dealing with the girls. The killing, the punishments, they made him so fucking happy. Energized him as nothing else could. And the preparation! He had a strong work ethic and spent so many years working for his girls to show them how much he loved them.

And now he's condemned to...this. He thought he'd be even stronger as a spirit. That he'd have more control. The fact that so many things he never considered could impact his energy only makes him angrier.

He hates feeling small.

That just won't do.

So, he decides to shift his focus.

He needs new toys.

He's starting to feel stronger now. The pain that rattles through this soul ebbs, and he can move again. There are spells to help him overcome this. He remembers reading about it in his mother's grimoire.

Of course, that's long gone in the fire.

They burned his house down.

The thought still fills him with so much rage. So much pain.

How dare they?

That's just one more thing he'll have to punish them for. Make them pay for destroying the one thing he worked so hard to give them. He left it all to them, didn't he? And they didn't want it.

They destroyed it.

He makes his way behind a mirror, weak and exhausted, and waits. It's a long wait this time, which only fuels his anger.

But when his new toy walks into the room—a bedroom this time—he fills with glee.

"Oh, look at you," he breathes. "Look at how perfect you are. With that long, red hair. Too curly to be my Daphne, but I'll forgive it. This time. Yes. Come this way. Come over here."

She walks to the dresser under the mirror, takes off her jewelry, and slips out of her shoes.

When she removes her sweater, he recoils in disgust when he sees the tattoos on her arms and back.

That won't do.

"Why would you mark yourself up like that?" he asks and watches as the toy frowns and looks around.

"Is someone there?" she calls out and listens. He sees just a hint of fear in her green eyes, and that pleases him.

Yes, that pleases him very much.

As much as he wants to kill her right away, to watch her scream and cry and beg as he has the right to, he's resigned himself to being patient with this one. He needs her energy. And he needs to teach them all a lesson.

"It's just the two of us," he says in a singsong voice. "I'm going to take very good care of you. Of course, before we're done, you'll have to lose those horrible tattoos. I don't know what you were thinking. But we'll fix it."

He longs for his electric chair. For his bench. For his favorite knife.

And feels the anger surge in him once more, gaining in strength again as he pulls energy from this new toy.

"Now, let's get started."

CHAPTER ELEVEN

Daphne

"Let's go check out where your new house will be," I suggest to Mama when the meeting comes to an end. "Let's talk about something fun for a bit."

"Oh, I'd love that," Mama says with a smile and then reaches out to take Miss Sophia's hand. "Thank you again for this."

"It's absolutely my pleasure. Let's go have a look, get the lay of the land, so to speak, and see what you think."

The guys are all huddled over some books at Miss Sophia's table, mumbling and talking. Lucien's parents, Oliver, and Miss Annabelle have all left.

Now it's time to take a breath and think about something *good*. Something that doesn't scare the hell out of me.

We set off down the little dirt road that winds away from Miss Sophia's cabin, through a little meadow, and then Miss Sophia gestures to her left.

"I was thinking this spot would be perfect," she says and takes Mama's hand to lead her into the meadow. "There are trees tucked here on the side for some good shade, but you'll also still have a view to my place. Our ritual field is even nearby."

"Oh, it's just lovely," Mama says with a contented sigh. "So peaceful. Can you feel it, girls? Take a deep breath."

We all breathe deeply, and I *do* feel it. The calm, the peace that rests here.

"I cleansed the area," Miss Sophia says. "It's a safe haven for you, Ruth."

"I'm so grateful," Mama says and swipes a tear off her cheek. "I don't think I can ever repay you for this."

"And there's no need to," Miss Sophia says simply. "Now, how do you want your place situated?"

"We were thinking two bedrooms," Millie says, walking farther into the meadow. "With a nice big bathroom that has a soaking tub. And a good-sized kitchen since you're a hedgewitch. You'll need plenty of working space."

"Oh, it's fun to think about, isn't it?" Mama says in delight. She's like a kid on Christmas morning. "Well, I think it would be lovely if the house faced toward yours, Miss Sophia. That would give a nice view of the meadow here, and the trees will be to the back of the house for shade. I could plant a garden right over there."

She walks and points, her eyes filled with excitement as she considers all the possibilities.

"I think that's a great idea," Brielle adds.

We spend a good half-hour making plans for Mama's new home and brainstorming ideas. When we walk back to see how the boys are doing, Mama slips her hand into mine and kisses my cheek.

"I love you, daughter."

I feel the tears and don't bother trying to blink them away.

I've waited my whole life to have a moment like this with my mother.

I smile over at her and soak in the pure happiness I see in her eyes. "I love you, too, Mama."

***

"WHY ARE YOU HERE?" Millie asks in surprise when I approach her at her counter at Witches Brew. Esme, her trusted employee, just grins at me. "Not that I'm not happy to see you. I just don't usually see you in the middle of a workday. Did you shut down the store?"

"Jack's there," I reply with a shrug. "I know I've been hesitant to bring on help in the past, but there's something to be said for leaving it in someone else's capable hands so I can go fetch a cup of coffee that I didn't have to make for myself."

Millie grins. "I love that he's there with you. That he's been staying *with* you."

"He's hot," Esme declares with a dramatic sigh. "Too bad he doesn't have a younger brother. I'm going to go straighten up the reading area."

She waves and hurries off to the back of the café where Millie has a little area set up for reading, working, or just sitting quietly.

"Please, *please* don't put any potions in my coffee," I plead with my sister, who simply raises an eyebrow.

"Why?"

"Because I just want *coffee*." I'm almost desperate when I reach over and cover her hand with mine. "No frills. No extras. Just coffee."

"As soon as we've put all of this craziness to bed, you can have as much plain coffee as you want. But for now, you need the extra protection. So, as long as I'm the one making it, that's how you'll drink it."

"You're mean."

I plop down onto a stool and sulk.

"No, I love you, and I'm looking out for you," she says and works her magic on my brew. Literally. She even waves her hand over it, whispering something. A little puff of smoke rises from it.

"Did you just poison me?"

She laughs and secures the lid, then frowns. "These lids have been wonky lately. Be careful, okay?"

"I've got it," I reply and take it from her. "It won't be in there long enough to worry about it. I think I'll stroll down to Mallory's shop and look for a few things before I head back to my place."

"That sounds fun." Millie waves as a couple of people walk into her café. "Tell her I said hello."

"Will do. Talk to you later."

I step out into the French Quarter and turn to walk the couple of blocks to Bayou Botanicals, our friend Mallory Boudreaux's business. She sells potions, crystals, oils, and all kinds of fun things. She's a member of Miss Sophia's coven and has been a good friend to us.

I push through her door and take a deep breath.

"It always smells so damn good in here."

Mallory's head turns at my voice, and she grins. "I have some new rosemary and lime soap. You should try it."

"Hell, yes, I should. Put me down for a bar. I'd also like some new crystals for my shop."

"Good idea." We spend a good amount of time sniffing and playing with lotions and oils. When she rings me up, I'm several hundred dollars poorer.

"Wow, we shopped like it's our job," I say as I pass her my card.

"It *is* my job," she says with a laugh.

"I guess it's mine, too, now that I think about it." I sign the slip and pass it back to her. "You have such awesome stuff in here, Mal."

"Thanks, I try."

"How's the family?"

Her smile spreads wider. "Beau's the best. He's home with the babies today because the nanny called in sick. So, he's working from home while they sleep."

"A billionaire hanging out with babies." I sigh and shake my head. "I think that might be the sweetest thing I've ever heard."

"I know, right?" She laughs and pushes her red hair over her shoulder. "I'm going to close early and go relieve him so he can get to the office. But everyone's doing well, thanks for asking. Having babies and making boats. Spending time at Inn Boudreaux out in the bayou."

"It's such a lovely place," I say, remembering the huge house the Boudreaux family converted into a bed and breakfast. "Gabby does a great job out there."

"We're having a little BBQ out there next week. There won't be any guests, and the weather is supposed to be cool. We'd love to have you. All of you."

"Oh. Well, thank you. That sounds like a lot of fun and something to distract us from... other things."

"I think so, too. I'll text you with the details."

"Sounds great." I take my bag of goodies and grin at the other woman. "I can't wait."

"I'll see you soon, then."

I wave and set off down the street, headed back to my car in front of Witches Brew. I *love* the French Quarter. It's so full of color. *Life.* The history is limitless. I've learned to keep my shields in place because of that vast history, but still, I love it.

I'm grateful to be able to live and work here.

I sip my coffee and grin.

I don't know what spell Millie casts on these so it stays warm until the last sip, but I love it.

I'm having a damn good day.

When I reach the car, I open the back door first to set my big bag in the back seat, and then I sit in the driver's seat and fasten my belt.

Only to look up into an eyeless face.

I scream, my coffee falling and spilling all over the front of me. It takes me a full twenty seconds to realize that what I'm staring at is a photo.

A polaroid.

"Fucking hell," I mutter and push my fingers into my eyes. "Scared the hell out of me."

I don't bother to take the photo out from beneath my windshield wiper. I don't want to touch it. Instead, I fire up the engine and call Cash.

"Hey, Daph."

"I'm staring at a photo of a woman with no eyes," I say by way of greeting. My heart still feels as if it's pounding out of my chest. "And I'm driving to you."

"Where are you?"

"Five minutes away. Meet me out front."

I do my best to ignore the face and the fact that I'm now wearing my delicious coffee, and hurry through traffic to the police department.

When I pull up out front, Cash is waiting for me on the steps.

"Jesus, why didn't you move it so you didn't have to stare at it?"

I shake my head as I get out of the car. "Because I don't want to touch it."

"Wait, do you see things when you touch the photos?"

I stop, suddenly stunned. "Actually, no. I don't see anything at all. I just feel the heartbeat. The warmth."

"That's creepy enough," he says grimly. "You haven't touched that at all?"

"Nope. It's a virgin, just waiting for you."

"Just like I like them—don't tell your sister I said that."

I grin and watch as he slips on gloves and gingerly takes the photo out from under the wiper blade.

He flips it over to look down at it.

"God, she's young."

"I noticed." I lean to look over his shoulder. Naked shoulders and her head are all that show in the black and white photo. "The timestamp."

"Tomorrow," he says with a nod. "He hasn't killed her yet."

"I hate this so fucking much," I growl. "I hate knowing that he has her, however that's possible, and is doing horrible things to her. That he's going to torture her and kill her. We don't know who she is, or how to find her. I hate feeling so helpless."

"I know," Cash says. "Trust me, I know. I'll run her. We might get lucky."

"I love your optimism."

"I'm going to do everything I can to find her before

he kills her," Cash promises and leans in to kiss my fore-head. "Should we call the others?"

"No."

I blow out a breath when he just raises his brows in surprise as if to say: *You'll be in trouble.*

"Seriously, this is starting to happen so often that if we get together every time, we'll *always* be together, and no one has time for that, Cash. I'm going back to work. I need to change these clothes and get on with my life."

"Okay. At least *tell* the others, Daph. They need to know."

"Yeah. I will. See you later."

I climb back into the car, relieved that the photo is gone. The drive to my shop takes longer than normal in traffic, and by the time I park in my spot and walk into Reflections, I'm in a very surly mood.

"Hey," Jack says with a grin but then sobers when he catches sight of me. "What happened?"

"I need to change," I reply and march straight into my office where I have a spare outfit waiting—just for times like this.

He follows me and doesn't turn away as I start to strip out of my soiled clothes.

He swallows hard when I'm down to my bra and panties.

He's been staying with me, *sleeping* with me for several days, but aside from some stolen kisses, there hasn't been any sex.

We're both exhausted, physically and emotionally, by the time we fall into bed.

But I can see by the light in his eyes that he'd like to change that very soon.

"Tell me what happened," he says.

"I got coffee at Witches Brew," I reply. "Went to see Mallory, picked up some fun things. We're going to Inn Boudreaux for a thing next week, by the way."

"A thing."

"That's right, a thing." My voice is snappy now, but I don't care. "Then I went back to my car, and there was a creepy-ass photo staring at me through the windshield. I'm getting really sick and tired of these photos, Jack. People missing their eyes is just...*wrong*."

"I won't argue that. Where's the picture?"

"I took it to Cash." I walk past him to the little kitchenette I have for coffee emergencies and start to make a cup.

"Without showing the rest of us?"

I scowl and wait impatiently for my coffee to brew.

"It's just like the others. Well, except he's not going to kill this one until tomorrow."

"Shit," he mutters and stalks around the kitchenette. "Male or female?"

"A woman." My voice is softer now. "She's pretty. And he's going to kill her. And, frankly, I'm sick to death of being scared. And worried. And drinking potions in my fucking coffee."

I pour cream into the brew, give it a quick stir, and take a sip.

"I'm tired of this, Jack. Of feeling like I'm walking on eggshells. Hell, I can't even walk through the French Quarter to buy some damn *soap* without him scaring the shit out of me. I dropped my coffee all over myself, and it was just awful. Millie insists I drink her potions, but I just want coffee. That's it. Just caffeine and angel tears in a cup."

"Okay."

He wraps his arms around me and cradles my head against his chest, clearly aware that I'm in the middle of a mental breakdown.

Jackson always did give the best hugs around.

"I'm sorry." He rocks me back and forth. "You're right. It's all bullshit. I hate that you're scared and being tormented. I want to hunt the bastard down and kill him all over again, just for that alone. It's not right."

"He ruined my morning." I sniff against him. "I was having a great day."

"You still will," he says and kisses my hair. "Especially when I tell you I sold that blue chair over there for the full asking price."

My eyes follow his hand, and I nod. "Yeah, that's good news. And I heard from the builder for Mama's house when I was on my way to Millie's earlier. They can start pouring the foundation next week."

"See? It's still a good day. Letting him mess everything up every time he does something like this is only making him happy," he reminds me. "Let's not give him that satisfaction."

"It might make him escalate," I warn him. "He tends to throw tantrums."

"I don't care about his tantrums. I care about you and your mental well-being."

"Which means I need coffee," I add and reach for the mug, taking a sip. "You know, Cash brought up a good point when I saw him. I told him I left the photo under the windshield wiper because I didn't want to touch it."

"Christ, you had to look at that while you drove?"

"Yeah, it sucked. Anyway, I don't see anything when I touch the photos. I feel the heartbeat and heat, which is so damn creepy I don't even want to think about it, but I don't have visions of anything like I do when I touch other things. Is he blocking me?"

"He might be," Jack says, thinking it over. "He might have cast some kind of spell on them so you can't see anything. He wouldn't want to be caught too soon."

"I'm going to have to touch the body," I say and set my mug aside. "When they find this new girl, I'm going to have to touch her."

"Why?" He brushes my hair away from my face, sending shivers through me.

The good kind.

"Because he's blocked me on the photos. But if I touch her, I might be able to see *him*. Or at least get a handle on some things. It helped when I touched one of the victims when he was still alive."

"I think that's too much, sweets," he says, shaking his head slowly. "It's too much to ask of you."

"No, it's not." I take his hand in mine. "Jack, if I can make this end, it's not too much at all. I'll do *anything* to get rid of him for good."

"I didn't think you could read people," he says with a scowl.

"I didn't think I could either," I say softly. "But nothing about this has been normal. Brielle saw full apparitions. Millie discovered all of her past lives with Lucien. It's all been anything *but* normal."

"I'm so sorry," he whispers and pulls me against him. Those strong arms wrap around me once more. "I think we need an evening that doesn't revolve around a paranormal serial killer."

"Oh, do tell."

I feel him smile against my hair.

"I'm going to make you dinner. And we're going to watch a movie, something light that will make you laugh. And then I'm going to draw you a hot bath to soak in."

"Well, that sounds pretty great." I sigh and sink into him. "Can I have bubbles in my bath?"

"You can have anything you want, sweets."

CHAPTER TWELVE

Jackson

"Maybe we should close the shop now and get started on the bubble bath early," Daphne suggests and hugs me closer, making me laugh.

"It's been steady in here this morning," I reply and kiss her head, then let her pull away from me. If I could, I'd keep my arms around her all the time. At least then, I'd know she's safe. "But if you want to play hooky, I'm always up for it."

"You, Jackson Pruitt, are a bad influence."

I grin and cross my arms over my chest. "I never claimed otherwise."

She giggles, and suddenly, the edges of my vision grow fuzzy. Gray.

"Just stay in bed," she coos and reaches for me with those talented hands as I slip out from under the covers. She falls face-down on the mattress when she misses me.

"You need coffee," I remind her. "And I know what your

wrath feels like when you're deprived of caffeine first thing in the morning."

"Well, yeah. Of course, I need coffee. But I could use something else first." She waggles her eyebrows and lets the blanket fall to reveal her plump, full breasts.

The breasts I enjoyed all night long.

I crawl back onto the mattress and sink into her plump lips, enjoying how she gives herself to me so completely and without qualms.

I'm about to say fuck the coffee and have her one more time when she suddenly pushes me back, her eyes wide, and hurries from the bed. She wraps her robe around herself and runs through the apartment.

"What's going on?" I demand, but she doesn't stop until she reaches the front door.

She pulls it open and then lets out a strangled gasp.

"Jack?"

I shake myself out of the vision. "What?"

"Your phone's ringing." Daphne scowls at me. "What did you see?"

I shake my head again and answer the phone. "Hello?"

"Hi there, Jackson. I know you're busy, and I don't want to interrupt anything important, but I wanted to talk to you for a minute about Oliver."

I frown at Miss Annabelle's statement. "You're never interrupting. What's wrong with Oliver?"

Daphne steps closer so she can hear the other end of the conversation.

"Well, he just doesn't look good, Jack. I asked him how he's feeling, and I can tell that it isn't great, but he's just too darn stubborn to go to the doctor. I was hoping you'd have a little time today to come and talk some sense into him."

"I'm on my way," I promise as Daphne immediately flips the *Open* sign to *Closed*. "We'll be there in just a little while. What's he doing now?"

"He's napping." I can hear tears in her voice. "I'm really worried about him."

"We'll get to the bottom of this. Daphne and I are on our way."

I end the call and send Daphne a grim look. "I'm sorry about this."

"Why on Earth are you sorry?" she asks and fetches her purse. "Oliver is your family. Let's go take care of it."

We rush out to my car, and I drive faster than I likely should through New Orleans, but the urgency to get to Oliver is a driving force in my gut.

Daphne reaches over and takes my hand in hers.

"He's going to be fine," she says with bright confidence. "We'll talk him into going to the doctor and get it all figured out."

I nod, turn into Oliver's driveway, and barely get the car parked and shut off before I'm rushing to the door of the house.

"Thank you for coming," Miss Annabelle says as she opens the door. "He's still asleep. He's been sleeping most of the morning."

"In the bedroom?" I ask.

"That's right. Go on in. It's okay."

I hurry to the back of the house and into the bedroom. Oliver is in bed, lying on his back. His breathing is shallow, and for a man with such dark skin, he's damn pale.

I sit on the edge of the bed and take his hand in mine. "Hey, Ollie. I need you to wake up for me."

His eyes flutter open, then close again as if he just can't fight against the sleep.

"Ollie, we need to get you to a doctor."

"I'm fine," he whispers through chapped lips.

"I don't think you are. We're all worried about you, and it'll make us feel a lot better if you get checked out. Miss Annabelle is worried sick. You don't want to make her fuss, do you?"

"Always fusses," he whispers. "Just tired."

I look up at Daphne, who hovers nearby. "Call an ambulance. It'll be safer."

"On it."

She pulls her phone out of her bag and calls emergency services as I watch Oliver slip back into a deep sleep.

"He's been like this all day," Miss Annabelle says as she takes his other hand and kisses his knuckles. "I couldn't get him to eat or drink anything at all."

"They're on their way. Five minutes," Daphne says. "I'm going to wait for them outside."

"Thank you," I reply.

"I'll go with you," Miss Annabelle says and hurries out of the room with Daphne.

"Too much fussin'," Oliver says, catching my attention. "Can't a man just sleep?"

"Not like this," I reply. "This isn't normal for you. I need to get you all checked out to make sure it's nothing serious. I've already lost two parents. I refuse to lose you, too."

A frown creases the area between his eyebrows, and then he just sighs.

"Fair enough, then."

It's not long before the ladies escort the EMTs into the room, and they immediately start asking questions.

How long has he been like this?

Is he on any medications?

Is he allergic to anything?

They load him onto a stretcher and take him out to the waiting ambulance. Miss Annabelle rides with them, and Daph and I follow closely behind.

"I've never seen him like that," I say and wipe my hand over my mouth in agitation. "Jesus, Daph, he looked half-dead."

"He looks exhausted," she corrects me. "Maybe it was something he ate or a medication he took too much of. It could literally be *anything*, Jack. Let's not freak out until we speak to the doctor."

I just nod and pull into the emergency room parking lot. We hurry inside, but the nurses tell us that we can't go back to his room until they get him settled.

I pace the waiting room.

Daphne calls her sisters.

Finally, close to an hour after we arrive, we're shown back to Oliver's room.

He's in a hospital gown with an IV in his arm, wires attached to his chest, and oxygen in his nose. The strong man I've known for all my life looks small and sick in that bed.

And everything in me goes stone-cold with fear.

"It looks worse than it is," Miss Annabelle is quick to say as she reaches for my hand. "They're running a few tests, but the doctor thinks he's just dehydrated and exhausted. Oliver's been working quite a lot and stays up late to read and research so he can try to help you two. He's worried."

"Lots of visitors."

We turn at the sound of the doctor's voice. She opens her laptop and smiles at all of us.

"I'm glad you brought Mr. Oliver in to see us today." She turns to the patient. "The blood tests show a little inflammation in your body. You're certainly dehydrated, which is dangerous by itself. I don't like the shallow breathing, but according to the chest x-ray, you don't have any pneumonia, so that's a good sign."

"Can I go home now?" Oliver asks.

"No way, José," the doctor says with a grin. "You're going to hang out here for a day or two so I can keep an eye on you. We'll keep pumping some fluids into you, get you to eat some of our delicious food, and get your strength up."

"I can do that at home."

"Not yet," the doctor says, just as stubborn as Oliver. "Don't worry, it's not so bad. Miss Annabelle can stay with you as long as she likes. We'll just get you up to a regular room and get you all settled in."

I shake my head when it looks as if Oliver might argue.

"You're staying put," I inform him. "If I have to stay with you and make sure you don't do anything stupid, I will."

Oliver doesn't slap back at me for that, which tells me he really doesn't feel well and is exactly where he needs to be.

"Fine." Oliver shifts in the bed. "I'll stay."

"Great," the doctor says. "I'll be back to check on you in a while. And after they take you upstairs, I'll look in on you up there, too."

"You don't have to do that," I say to her. "I know that's not usual."

"I like him," is all she says before leaving the room.

"Already charming the hospital staff," Daphne says with a wink for Miss Annabelle. "What can we bring you?"

"Oh, I think I'm fine for now, thank you." Miss Annabelle leaves Oliver's side long enough to give me a big hug. "You're a good boy."

I laugh and kiss her cheek. "I've got you fooled."

"You can't fool me," she says and pats my cheek. "Now, you two go back to doing whatever I interrupted. We'll be just fine here. I have my cross-stitch, and I'll keep my eye on this one."

We say our goodbyes, and I promise to come back in the morning to check on things. When we're in my car, Daphne sighs.

"You know what?" she says and glances my way. "I know it's barely two in the afternoon, but it feels like we've already lived through a whole day. I want a glass of wine."

"Your wish is my command."

SHE DRANK the wine while I made the tacos. And then we curled up in her living room to watch an old Chevy Chase movie and eat chips and guacamole until we felt like bursting.

"Would you eat the last apple?" I ask her as the credits roll, and she stands to take our mess into the kitchen. I grab some glasses and plates and follow her.

"What?"

"If we were stuck somewhere overnight, hungry and cold, and you only had one measly apple, would you keep it for yourself or share it with me?"

She laughs and rinses a plate before stacking it in the dishwasher.

"We're not living in *Funny Farm*. But, no, I wouldn't be stingy. I would share."

"I might not share," I admit and then laugh when her jaw drops, and she stares at me in horror. "What? It's just an apple."

"Never mind, then. I'm not sharing either." She firms her lips and shakes a glass at me. "You can just fend for yourself, Jackson Pruitt. You and your self-ishness."

I take the glass from her grasp and set it aside, then pull her against me and kiss her long and slow, just soaking her in. When I pull back to take a breath, she murmurs, "I don't kiss men who don't share."

I chuckle and kiss her once more. "Okay, I'd probably share with you. If you asked nicely. Now, I promised you a bath."

"A *bubble* bath," she reminds me and lets me lead her to the bathroom. "Oh, wait. I got you something today. I almost forgot."

She hurries to a bag on the dining room table and comes back holding a little brown pouch.

She shakes the contents into my hand, and I stare down at the pendant on a silver chain.

"We all wear our stones," she says softly. "Mine is rose quartz. For harmony, love, and trust. It's a healing stone. With our stones—my sisters and mine—and now Cash's and Lucien's—"

"The guys wear them, too?"

"Of course. Lucien has always worn black onyx, but

Brielle finally convinced Cash to wear his amethyst, as well. He just wears it under his shirt. Anyway, they've all been cast with a protection spell, cleansed, and charged. And I had the same done for this one. I know it looks purple, but it's not amethyst. It's auralite. For—"

"Also for healing," I interrupt, turning the stone over in my palm. "For calm. Relieves tension and strain and can even soothe a hot temper."

"It soothes and heals the *mind*," she says as she slips it out of my hand and over my head. "And with your visions, I thought this was appropriate. I know they're getting worse. I can feel the tension in you when you've had them. I want you to wear this, all the time, to keep you safe."

"Thank you." I brush my fingertips over the smooth stone, and then over hers. "So, you're letting me hang out with you a lot."

I tick items off on my fingers.

"You let me kiss you, you're *worried* about me, and now you're buying me gifts."

"Do you have a point?" She raises a brow, but there's humor in her gorgeous eyes.

"You love me."

Surprise replaces the humor, and then she starts to raise that wall of defense she's so good at when it comes to me. I frame her face in my hands.

"It's okay that you love me, Daphne. And I'll tell you why."

She grips my wrists and watches me avidly.

"Because I love you so much it hurts. I feel like I've loved you all of my life. As if I were just waiting until I met you. And then those years without you were just plain torture. Living without you was way worse than surviving any war zone. I love you, and I'm never going to do anything so stupid that it drives a wedge between us again. I can't promise to never make mistakes, but I can tell you that I'll never walk away."

She narrows those eyes and then sighs.

"I never *stopped* loving you, you big oaf. I wanted to. Trust me, I did. But I couldn't. You're meant for me. And for a while, that meant living through the pain of it. So, yeah, I love you. I bought you a protection pendant, didn't I?"

"Yeah." I kiss her nose. "You did."

"Let's not get all mushy about it."

I laugh and lead her into her bathroom, turning on the bathwater and dropping in some bubbles.

"Fine, we won't get mushy. But I'm telling you, here and now, that once you get naked, you're not getting *un*naked for the rest of the day."

A slow smile spreads across her beautiful face.

"Deal. But first, I need this bath. Mostly because I have to shave my legs. It's been a while. I've been busy."

I laugh but shrug and leave her to her bath while I clean the kitchen. I can hear her splashing away in there, talking to herself. She hums for a while.

With the kitchen back to the way I found it, I walk

into the bedroom and take off my shoes, then turn down the bed.

I've never been so nervous in my life.

I've had sex with this woman before—plenty of times. Hell, we were each other's firsts, way back in the day. I knew her body better than I knew mine back then.

Knew.

That's the keyword. Because it's been a hell of a long time.

I'm down to my underwear when I hear footsteps behind me. I turn and just about swallow my tongue.

Standing there in the doorway is Daphne. Completely naked, aside from the pendant she never takes off.

Her long, curly red hair falls around her shoulders, and her brilliant dark eyes are glued to mine.

That gorgeous pale skin of hers looks soft from her bath, and my God, I fucking want her.

"Getting a little cold over here," she says as goose-bumps form over her skin.

"I can fix that."

I scoop her up and tumble her into bed, rolling her beneath me as I kiss her like my life depends on it.

Because right this minute, it feels like it does.

Her nails scrape down my back, her legs skimming up mine and coming to rest over my hips.

It would be *so* easy to just slip right inside of her and take her.

But I'm not here for easy. Definitely not this time.

So, despite her delectable invitation, I slow down and slide my nose over the skin of her neck and up to her ear as I whisper, "You're the sexiest thing I've ever seen in my life."

She smiles, and those hands tighten on my shoulders.

"But," I continue, "we're going slow here, sweets."

"We can do slow later," she offers. "Fast now, slow later."

"Slow now, slow later."

She narrows her eyes, and I laugh, then fasten my lips over one of her nipples. She sighs and shoves her fingers into my hair.

"See? It's a good idea."

"What about slow now, fast later, then slow later-later."

My head comes up in surprise. "You're trying to kill me."

She giggles and then sighs again when my lips travel down to her navel. Her skin smells like lavender and lemon and feels like fucking heaven.

I've dreamed of her like this for years.

I never thought I'd be back here.

I lean my forehead against her belly, her hips in my hands, and simply stop to rest and take a breath.

"What's wrong?" she asks and combs her fingers in my hair once more. God, she's good at that.

"I just missed you," I murmur and then look up at her. "I missed everything about you."

She curls up, cups my cheek, and presses her lips to mine so sweetly it makes my heart ache. Her lips are soft and pliable, and when she moans in that light way she does, I press her back down and return to the task at hand.

Making her fucking crazy.

CHAPTER THIRTEEN

Daphne

Was it always this intense? Before, when we were so young and so ridiculously in love with each other, was it this intense when we made love?

Because this is way better than I remember.

Maybe it's good that I don't remember it being this way because it would have only pissed me off more.

I can't stop combing my fingers through his soft hair. He presses a sweet kiss to my stomach, and the butterflies there go absolutely *crazy*.

The room is cool, thanks to a landlord that believes in a good air-conditioning unit, and Jack's skin is warm against me, his mouth hot as he leaves open-mouthed kisses over my body.

I take a deep breath and let myself close my eyes and simply *feel* him. Enjoy how he makes me feel—so sexy and alive. My body hums with excitement, and my heart swells with more love than I knew was possible.

When he slides over me, links his hand with mine, and unites us, the lights flicker around us—just the way they used to *before*.

My eyes meet his as he smiles.

The lights get crazier as he picks up the tempo.

I bite his shoulder.

He growls in my ear.

And the world explodes around us in a wave of pure, wild lust.

"I think we broke the lightbulb in the bathroom," I mutter, struggling to catch my breath.

"I'll replace it," he says before rolling over and pulling me with him. He tucks me against his chest. "In about ten years, when I can move again."

"It's crazy to me that we always made the lights do that." I let my fingers drift up and down his hard, flat stomach. "I'm not able to do that any other time."

"Me, either." He kisses my forehead. "Are you hungry?"

I lift my head in surprise. "Are *you* hungry? I ate enough tacos earlier to feed Mexico."

He smirks. "You always were a little dramatic."

I narrow my eyes and pinch his side, making him yelp. "Why does everyone say that? I'm literally *not* dramatic."

He laughs and pulls me against him, even when I try to half-heartedly fight him off—just out of principle.

"Right. You're not dramatic. Okay."

"You know what? You're a smartass. No more blowjobs for you, ever again."

"Okay, there's no need to take it that far."

I laugh when he rolls me onto my back and then sigh when he kisses my neck in that spot that makes my toes curl.

"What do you say we make the lights flicker again?" he asks.

"I thought you were hungry."

"I am." His tongue traces the outside of my ear. "For you."

I WAKE to the bed moving, and the blankets shifting. I crack one eye to see Jackson ease his way out of bed and have a spectacular view of his very fine ass.

"Just stay in bed." I reach for him, but I miss and fall with my face in the mattress.

"You need coffee," he says, grinning down at me in that very pleased way men do when they know they've spent the better part of the night before rocking your world. "And I know what your wrath feels like when you're deprived of caffeine first thing in the morning."

"Well, yeah, of course I need coffee. But I could use something else first." I waggle my eyebrows and send him a come-hither look as I sit up and let the blankets fall to my hips, revealing my breasts.

Jackson always was a boob man.

He crawls back onto the bed, like a wolf stalking its prey, and kisses me like crazy. Suddenly, overpowering nausea moves through me from head to toe.

I push him away and hurry from the bed, grabbing my robe on the way from the bedroom to the front door and wrapping it around me.

"What's going on?" Jackson asks as he runs behind me, but I can't speak.

I have to get to the front stoop.

I yank open the door and gasp when I see that I'm right.

Another envelope.

"Damn it," he mutters from behind me as I reach down for the photo. "I guess the fun and games are over."

I sigh, and with the envelope gripped between my thumb and forefinger, walk into the living room.

"It was nice to forget for a little while," I say with a sigh. "Thanks for giving me that."

He sits next to me and takes my other hand. "Go ahead."

I nod once and then pull the photo out of the envelope, feeling nausea roll through me once more.

"Oh, Goddess. I know him."

"What?" Jackson takes the photo and examines it. "You know this man?"

"Yes. I mean, with the eyes gone, it's hard to tell for sure, but I'm pretty sure that's Caleb Browning. He's part of the coven up in Baton Rouge. Jackson, I *know* him."

"We have to call the others," he says as he looks around frantically for his phone. He finally finds it in the bedroom, and I hear him talking as he pulls on some clothes. "Another picture. She says she knows him. A Caleb Browning? Yeah, we'd appreciate it. See you soon."

He returns from the bedroom but veers into the kitchen to make some coffee.

"The timestamp," I mutter, noticing it for the first time. "Jack, this one is just a few minutes after the other one—on the photo I found yesterday."

"Cash is bringing it," he informs me. They're all on their way over."

"I'd better get dressed."

I take the offered mug of caffeine from Jack and walk into the bedroom, where I take just a moment to breathe. To remember last night and how wonderful I felt for those few hours when nothing mattered except the man I love.

It was glorious.

The rumpled bed is evidence of that.

I take a bolstering sip of the brew and then get dressed. I've just stepped out of the bedroom when the others file into my apartment.

"Well, good morning," Millie says with a wink. She leans in to whisper in my ear. "There is so much sexual energy flying around this place, it might burn something."

"It was a fun night," I reply with a shrug and then laugh when my sister just grins at me.

"Let me see the photo," Lucien demands, and I pass it over to him.

"You know Caleb better than I do," I say as he examines it. "Am I wrong?"

"No." His face is grim as he looks up at me. "You're not wrong. This is him. I recognize the scar by his mouth."

"The timestamp on it is just a few minutes after the one from yesterday," I say as Cash steps forward with the other photo. "This afternoon."

"Oh, God," Lucien breathes. "This is Steph. She and Caleb are matched. They're a couple."

His eyes meet mine.

"No. Oh, Goddess, no. Why didn't I show everyone the photo yesterday? I'm so stupid."

"You didn't know," Brielle says and rubs big circles on my back.

"And we can't change it," Cash adds. "But maybe we can get to them before Horace kills them."

"Do we know where they live?" Brielle asks.

"Honey, we can find out in a matter of seconds," Cash says with a grin and starts tapping on his phone.

"Baton Rouge," Lucien says, pacing the living room. Caleb and Lucien are friends. They've known each other for a long time. "They just moved in together. Into Steph's house. I don't know the address."

"I've got it," Cash announces. "Let's move."

"It's more than an hour away," Millie reminds us. "Shouldn't we call in the local authorities?"

"If they're going to kill themselves," Cash says, "the authorities won't listen to me. I've run up against nothing but a wall with them on this."

It's the longest drive of my life. Lucien's been trying to call Caleb the entire trip, but the other man doesn't answer.

Finally, we pull into a driveway, and all of us burst out of the car, hurrying up the front porch with Cash in the lead.

He bangs on the door. "Stephanie? Caleb? I need you to open this door. My name is Cash. I'm with the New Orleans PD, and I need to speak with you."

More pounding, but no one answers.

"Fuck this," Lucien growls. "Open the goddamn door."

Cash breaks it open, and we rush inside, then stop cold at the scene before us.

"No one move," Cash says quietly.

"Make it stop." Caleb is systematically peeling off Stephanie's skin. The woman is clearly already dead. He's weeping, his face contorted in pain, his expression tortured. "Get him out of my head. I can't stop. Oh, God."

Lucien and Millie immediately start a spell,

chanting together and holding hands. Jackson joins them. I don't know how he knows the words, but he joins them.

Cash approaches Caleb and gently takes the knife away from the other man. There's suddenly wind in the room, a scream, and then calm.

"I couldn't stop," Caleb says. "He was in my head, and he wouldn't let go. He wouldn't *stop*."

He sits on the couch, his head in his hands, and continues weeping.

I rush to the kitchen and fill a glass with water, bringing it to him as I sit next to him.

The couch. It's full of fun memories—making love and laughter. Watching TV shows together.

A proposal just a week ago.

Oh, Goddess, *why*?

"He made me," he says through tears. "Said he didn't like the tattoos. Her beautiful ink."

He looks over to where the woman lies on the floor, surrounded by blood, missing half of her skin.

"Oh, God. I killed her."

"Okay, Caleb, look at me." Lucien squats in front of him and rests his hand on his shoulder. "This isn't your fault. Horace used *your* body to hurt her. You didn't do this. It wasn't you."

"It was my hands," Caleb insists. "My hands did this to her. She was sweet and good, and she didn't deserve to die like that."

"No," Lucien agrees. "She didn't. I'm so sorry, my

friend. But I'm telling you the truth. This isn't your fault."

"We're going to destroy this fucker," Jackson says, his voice hard as stone. "He's going to suffer for this."

"It doesn't matter." Caleb's eyes are glassy now with shock. "Oh, God, it doesn't matter. She's gone. My girl is gone."

He dissolves into tears once more. Cash is on the phone with the local authorities. Millie and Brielle are talking softly nearby.

I don't know what to do.

If only I'd shown that photo to Lucien, we might have been able to stop this.

It's not Caleb's fault at all.

It's mine.

———

"I DOUBT HE'LL BE CHARGED," Cash says later when we're all gathered at Millie and Lucien's house. He looks as if he's aged ten years just today alone. "I finally got through to someone in homicide who's been following what's been going on here. Thank Christ."

"He'll need some serious help," I murmur and rub my face. "I'm so sorry. I'm so, so sorry. I don't know how to make this right. I should have shown the photo to everyone yesterday. I was just so irritated and tired. And I was selfish. It's that simple. And because I was, she's dead, and Caleb will likely be traumatized for life."

"You didn't know," Lucien says, his face full of grief. "You didn't know, Daph."

"I was *selfish*," I repeat. "Oh, Goddess, I can't imagine it. If he made me do that to Jackson, I couldn't bear it. I couldn't survive it."

"Stop." Brielle's voice is firm. "Stop it, Daphne. Beating yourself up over this isn't helping anything or anyone. It isn't going to *solve* anything. You didn't mean to make the oversight. You don't have a malicious bone in your body. No one blames you."

I blame me.

But I stay quiet and lean into Jackson. Let him squeeze my hand.

"I think he's going after coven members," Lucien says thoughtfully and absently reaches over to pet Sanguine, Millie's feline familiar. The calico stretches and purrs under Lucien's hand. "I've done some research on the other two bodies we found. Both were members of a coven."

"Did you know them?" I ask.

"No, I didn't recognize them or their names. But they're members of covens that ours sometimes partners with. Caleb and Steph came to help us in the bayou when we burned down Horace's house."

"Is that where you knew him from?" Jack asks me.

"Yeah, I recognized him. But he and Lucien have been friends for a long time. I've seen him around, even though I haven't been a practicing witch since the day you walked out my door."

Jackson's eyes go dark. "You never told me that before."

I shrug a shoulder. "It doesn't really matter. I just stopped. But we have mutual friends, and Millie. So, I move in the same circles. I knew as soon as I saw that photo that it was Caleb."

"Okay, why is he targeting witches?" Brielle asks.

"Because he's trying to diminish our army," Millie replies. "If he eliminates those witches, the ones that would come and help us, we'll be weaker when the time comes."

"That son of a bitch," Jackson mutters.

"We need to get the word out," Millie says. "Everyone needs to get their protection spells in place. Goddess, we need to *protect* everyone."

"It's already happening," Lucien replies. "I spoke with Miss Sophia."

"I want extra protection on her," I say, surprising the others. "No one is as powerful as Miss Sophia. Everyone knows that she is our guide, and I want to be sure that he can't touch her."

"Would he dare try?" Brielle asks. "I know he's a psychopath, but hear me out. He's no stranger to witchcraft. He was part of a dark coven his entire life. He knows how powerful Miss Sophia is. Would he try to go up against her?"

"He's got an ego the size of the moon," Millie reminds her. "Yes, I think he would. I think he'll try to get to anyone who might try to help us. You guys, I'm even more convinced that we should all be together under one roof. We are exponentially stronger together, and we all know that. Please, please stay here. We have more space than we know what to do with."

"I'll stay," I say softly, again surprising the ones I love. "I'm scared. I'm not convinced the protection spells on my place have kept him out, and I want to make sure *you're* all safe. If we're better together, then we should be together."

"Agreed," Brielle says.

The men nod in agreement, as well.

"Starting today," Millie adds. "Go gather your things and bring them here. I've just finished furnishing all the rooms, so there are plenty of beds."

"What about our jobs?" I ask. "We can't just sit here until the eclipse."

"No one is ever alone," Lucien says.

"I'm fine working at Reflections with Daphne," Jackson adds.

"And I always have Esme at the shop," Millie adds. "Along with Gwyneth part-time."

"I'm taking a leave of absence from my lab," Lucien announces. "Until this is wrapped up, I'll be doing research and everything else I need to do in order to make sure we don't fail. I'll be able to do the bulk of my work from Witches Brew."

"I'm literally never alone on my ghost tour," Brielle says. "I'm booked solid. There will be at least twenty people with me every evening."

"And I'll come along," Cash says before kissing his wife's cheek.

"What about you, Cash?" I ask him.

"I'm a cop."

"You're a *man*. One of the six. You can't be alone, either."

He blows out a breath. "The eclipse is less than two weeks away. I'll talk to my boss about also taking a little time. He knows what we're up against. I don't think he'll balk."

"Good." I sigh in relief and look at each of them, one by one. "I love you all so much. And we've already been through hell and back with this. We've defeated him twice. I promise we won't fail this time."

"No, we won't." Jack kisses my hand. "Who's going to call Miss Sophia and talk her into staying with us for a while?"

"That means Mama's coming, too," Brielle says with a sigh. "It'll be a full house."

"It's a big house," Millie says, reminding us all. "We'll make it work."

"I think Millie should talk to Miss Sophia," I say and grin when my sister turns wide eyes to me.

"Why *me*?"

"Because you're her favorite. And she's your great-granddaughter. Tell her she either does what you say, or she gets a time-out."

"I don't think it works that way," Millie says with a laugh. "I don't think I can put Miss Sophia in time-out."

"I was kidding—sort of. But you *are* her favorite, and she *is* your great-granddaughter. She'll listen to you. Just be honest. Explain our fears."

"Daphne's right, my love," Lucien says. "I won't let him get to her."

"Agreed." Millie sighs. "Okay, I'll talk to her. But she's stubborn."

"So are you," I remind her.

CHAPTER FOURTEEN

"Violent delights tend to have violent ends."
-Richard Ramirez, The Night Stalker

"Those little bitches," he growls after he picks himself up from being thrown out of his play-time with his toys. They just marched right in and *threw him out*.

"They think they're so smart," he says. He has to curl up into a tight little ball because they zapped so much of his energy. The *new* energy that he'd just pulled from his toy.

The skin peeled away so beautifully. It hadn't been the first time he'd wished he could do it himself, with his own two hands, but watching was its own kind of beauty. She'd bled out sooner than he would have liked, but still, it was a masterpiece.

They interrupted him before he could finish with the other toy. The six were together now, and they cast a *spell* on him.

How dare they? Why did they refuse to understand —to believe—that everything he did, every single thing, was for his girls?

"Those *men* are brainwashing them," he mutters in disgust. "Women are so weak. So easy to manipulate. I have to get rid of the men, and then I'll be able to get through to my girls. Make them understand. I got rid of Jackson once. Killed his parents, and made him *go*. I can do it again. I can get through to all of them."

Happy with that plan, he moves to his special mirror, the one he's gained most of his energy from. When he has to wait much longer than ever before, he grows impatient.

"Where is he?" Horace complains but waits some more.

Hours later, when the toy hasn't returned, Horace punches at the glass and surprises himself when it breaks.

He's weak.

He has to find more energy.

So, he leaves the mirror and decides to start early with the next toy.

But when he tries to slip into those mirrors, a

powerful spell blocks him. He tries again and again, but every mirror he attempts is protected.

Rage surges with an energy all its own.

"How *dare* they?" he demands, baring his teeth.

This won't do.

This won't do at all.

Now he has to teach them a new lesson and search for another toy. One who isn't connected to a coven. A random plaything.

But as an idea takes shape in his mind, he calms.

Oh, yes. This will be a delight.

CHAPTER FIFTEEN

Jackson

"Your room is on the main floor," Millie says to Miss Sophia after they tour the house.

Honestly, I'm shocked that she agreed to stay. The fact that she did tells me that the thing we're up against is scarier than any of us wants to admit.

"Oh, this is lovely," I hear Miss Sophia say as they walk into a room off the kitchen. "You didn't have to put fresh flowers in here."

Daphne and I share a smile.

Of course, we did. Butter her up a bit.

"We're just so happy you're here," Millie says. "I know it's a full house of people, but it won't be for long. I want to keep you safe."

"Ruth and I will be just fine," Miss Sophia says as the three of them come into the kitchen. "I didn't agree to come because I'm afraid for us."

Ruth pours herself a cup of tea and takes a seat next to Daphne at the bar.

"Then why?" Millie asks.

"Because I fear there's more to know, more to learn than I originally thought. We've only scratched the surface. And now that he's targeting witches, it sends this whole thing into a new ballgame, so to speak. I'll be busy with research, but I also want to keep my eye on you girls. And Ruth, as well."

"There's safety in numbers," Ruth adds. "It's smart to be together. Where are Brielle and Cash?"

"They just left a bit ago to get started on her first ghost tour of the day," I reply. "Cash will be with her at work every day until this is over."

"Good," Miss Sophia says. "I don't want any of you alone."

"We have the library set up as a workspace," Millie says. "There are some extra desks in there, as well. It seems appropriate, and I really like the atmosphere in there."

"Well, that makes sense," Miss Sophia says with a soft smile. "I've heard stories about the many hours you spent in the library during your last lifetime."

It's still so weird to me to think that Millie and Lucien lived in this very house a hundred years ago in a previous life.

And that Miss Sophia is their direct descendent from that time.

It's just...*crazy*.

My phone pings with a text.

Miss A: *Hello, darlin'. Oliver and I can go home today. Would you be able to drive us?*

Me: *Of course. I'll head that way now.*

"Oliver's being released from the hospital." I stand and lean over to kiss Daphne's cheek. "I'm going to go take him and Miss Annabelle home."

"I'll go with you," Daphne says, standing with me.

"You don't have to—"

"No one goes alone, remember?" Daphne winks and glances at Millie. "Do you need us to stop and grab anything for dinner?"

"Oh, no, I have everything," Millie says. "Be safe out there."

We have to fight traffic to get to the hospital. When we finally walk into Oliver's room, he's dressed and ready to go.

"Perfect timing," Miss Annabelle says with a smile. With her big handbag on her arm, she gestures for us to go.

Oliver looks fantastic. I don't remember the last time I saw him looking so energized. So *young*.

"Wow, did they give you a sip of water from the fountain of youth?" I ask him. "You look great."

"Feel fit as a fiddle," he replies with a smile as a pretty nurse pushes his wheelchair. "Guess I need to drink more water."

"That's it?"

"Seems so," Oliver replies. "Hooked me up to that

IV thing for a couple of days, and today, I feel so much better."

"Well, it's good to see you looking healthier," Daphne says as she pats Oliver's shoulder. "I was worried about you."

"All these pretty girls, worried about little ol' me."

Oliver preens as we take the elevator down, and they all wait for me at the hospital entrance as I hurry to get the car.

"Does anyone else feel like some beignets?" Oliver asks us all.

"His appetite is back," Miss Annabelle says with a smile. "Darlin', you can have whatever you like."

"Then beignets it is," Oliver says. "As long as y'all don't have nowhere else to be."

"No, sir, we're all yours," Daphne says and sends me a smile.

God, I love her. How did I ever think I could live without her?

The wait for Café du Monde is relatively short. Before long, we're seated at a table in the shade with cold coffees and a platter full of fried dough covered in powdered sugar between us.

Oliver doesn't wait even a minute. He just digs in, enjoying them as if he hasn't had them in years.

"I never get tired of these," Daphne says with a sigh and wipes powdered sugar off her cheek.

"What's been happening with you two?" Miss

Annabelle asks. "Have there been any new developments?"

I share a look with Daph and then fill them in on the past twenty-four hours, keeping it as undescriptive as possible.

"He's going after our own," Oliver says softly. "Well, I'll be damned."

"We've spread the word to the others," Daphne says, keeping her voice low so the patrons at the other tables can't hear. "And they're doing what they need to do in order to keep themselves safe. We're all staying at Millie's house because it's huge, and we just think it's safer to all stay in one place."

"Smart," Oliver says, nodding. "That's real smart."

"I hope you don't mind," I add, ready to take Miss Annabelle's wrath, "but I had Miss Sophia and Millie walk through your house today to cast more protection spells and lay some fresh stones. I won't take any chances with the two of you."

"I don't mind a bit," Miss Annabelle says. "Thank you for thinking of it. I'll do some more things after we get home and settled. I have my mama's grimoire. It has some good old spells in it that I'll cast, as well."

"How are we going to get through between now and the eclipse?" Daphne asks. "It feels like an eternity. And I'm afraid he's just going to keep torturing and killing innocent people. If he can't get to the coven members, he'll turn to someone else."

"You're doing all you can," Oliver reminds her. "This

has been in the works for a damn long time. It won't be resolved in a day. You'll live your life—carefully. You'll learn. And by the goddess, you'll stay safe. That's the most important thing."

"It's sad what happened to Caleb and his girl," Miss Annabelle says softly. "I like him very much. Didn't know her all that well, but she seemed mighty nice."

"This has to stop," I murmur and reach for Daphne's hand. "It's time for it to end."

The drive to Oliver and Miss Annabelle's house is more somber than before, but when I come to a stop outside of their place, Oliver grins.

"No place like home," he says and climbs out of the car.

I walk up beside him, and he rests his arm across my shoulders.

"Sure do love you," he says. Oliver's never been one to shy away from the way he feels.

"Same here, old man. Don't pull that crap on me again."

Oliver laughs, and Miss Annabelle pulls her phone out of her purse.

"My boys." She sniffles just a little. "I need a picture of my boys. Smile at me now. Ah, there we go. I'm fixin' to frame this one."

"I'd love a copy of that," Daphne says as the two women walk into the house ahead of us.

Before we can follow them, Oliver tugs me back.

"I have a bad feeling," he says quietly. "I don't want

Annabelle to hear me say this because I don't want to scare her, but I have a real bad feeling. I need you to watch out for yourself and for Daphne. I know this is going to be tough, and we'll be there every step of the way to help, but I want your word that you'll be extra cautious, Jackson."

I've never heard fear in Oliver's deep voice before.

"You have my word," I reply earnestly. "And the same goes. I want you and Miss Annabelle to be safe, as well. If this isn't where you should be, there's one more bedroom at Millie's."

"We're okay here," he says and pats me on the shoulder. "But I want you to check in with me every day. I promised your daddy I'd take care of you, and I'll be damned if this son of a bitch stops me from keeping my word."

"I'll check in. I promise. Now, let's get in there before Miss Annabelle comes looking for us."

When we walk into the house, Miss Annabelle already has a frying pan on the stove in the kitchen, and she's getting ready to cook.

"I'm making y'all a meal," she says with a smile. "You're not getting out of here without some food in your belly."

"No, that would be a travesty, given that we just ate a bunch of beignets," I say with a laugh and then duck out of the way when she raises her hand to me. Not that she's ever laid a hand on me. "You wouldn't hit me."

Daphne and Oliver are in the living room, chatting. I can hear their low voices.

"How can I help?" I ask the woman who's become a mother to me. "I know my way around a kitchen."

"You can just sit and talk with me," she says with a smile. "How are you doing? How are things with you and that precious girl?"

"We're doing great." I reach over to snatch a cucumber out of the salad she's making. "I'm going to marry her."

Miss Annabelle looks up at me, her face softening in a smile. "You wait right here."

She wipes her hands on a towel as she hurries out of the kitchen. In then less than a minute, she returns carrying a small box.

"I can finally give this back to you."

I flip open the lid and look down. "My mom's engagement ring."

"You gave that to me for safekeeping after things fell apart before, and you decided to pursue different things," she says quietly and rubs her hand up and down my arm. "But it's time you have it back. When the time's right, offer it to that girl of yours."

"Thank you." I lean in to kiss her cheek. "Thanks for keeping it safe for me."

"You know there's not much we wouldn't do for you, my boy." She pats my cheek and then gets back to work. "Now, let's get this food ready. I have people to feed."

"I WANT TO TALK TO YOU." We just drove away from Oliver's, headed back to Millie's, and I have about twenty minutes alone with Daphne.

I need to get something off my chest.

"I'm right here," she says and shifts in her seat to face me. "What's up?"

"You said before that you stopped practicing witchcraft the day I walked out."

She doesn't say anything.

"Why, Daph?"

"Because it was tied to *you*," she says. "Because I met you the day I went with Millie to my first coven meeting. And, honestly, I didn't want to run into you there. I didn't know what was happening—if you were staying or leaving. I knew *nothing*. But I sure didn't want to chance seeing you there. I was too raw, and I knew I'd make a dramatic scene or something. Even though I'm *not* dramatic."

"I never went back either," I reply and feel myself settle when she reaches for my hand. "I packed my shit and enlisted. I wanted out of here. It was like a driving force, *making* me go. I couldn't leave fast enough."

"I wasn't a very good witch anyway. I never did the homework. I couldn't cast a spell if my life depended on it. And right now, it kind of does." She clears her throat. "Miss Annabelle gave me some clippings off her plants, and a bracelet that she says was her mother's lucky charm. They're worried about us."

"Yeah, I know. But don't change the subject."

She laughs a little. "I'm not. There's not much more to say."

"Did you miss it?"

"Some of the people, yes. I did. But I saw most of them anyway because of Millie. I'm not lying when I say I wasn't good at it, Jack. I always felt like an imposter, so it was easy to stop going. To just let that part of me slip away."

"You were never an imposter." I glance her way and squeeze her hand. "Not everyone is super-gifted like Miss Sophia, Daph. Her knowledge comes from a literal lifetime of studying and honing her craft."

"I know," she says. "But it just comes so naturally to Millie."

"And now we know that Millie has been honing *her* craft over a millennium."

"You have a point. But she says that we've *all* lived through the same lifetimes. So, wouldn't that mean I should have been learning over a millennium, too?"

"No. Because she said there were many times that you and Brielle didn't believe or understand. It was always part of Millie's path, not yours."

"So, our defeating *him* this time isn't necessarily linked to the coven," she says, thinking it over. "Yet he's targeting coven members? That doesn't make sense."

"Only with the aid of the craft will we be able to defeat him," I reply and park in front of Millie's house. Neither of us makes a move to leave the car. "He's too powerful an entity at this point to even try to defeat him in any other way. In fact, there probably *isn't* another way."

"Good point."

"And he knows that. So, yeah, he's taking out our army. And that really pisses me off, Daph."

"I know." She pulls my hand to her face and nuzzles her cheek against it. "I know it does. We're going to figure all of this out, Jack. One more thing about me being part of the coven... I've been considering going back to it. Since all of this started happening, it's been really nice to have a close community around us. And I find a lot of it fascinating, even if I'm not especially gifted at it."

"It just takes time," I repeat. "And if you want to practice magic, who am I to say that you shouldn't?"

"Would *you* consider going back?"

I lick my lips, thinking it over. "I think so. I don't have anything against it. I just couldn't stay with it back then. It was too painful because my parents loved it so much."

"I know. And I'm not saying you have to because I want to."

"No." I lean over and kiss her gently. "You wouldn't say that. I think it's something to think about."

Someone knocks on the window, startling us both.

"Stop making out in the driveway and come in for dinner," Brielle says and gestures for us to come inside.

"I guess she's home from work," Daphne mutters. "Although, I'm not hungry. Between beignets and Miss Annabelle cooking enough for an army, I may never eat again."

"Let's go in with the others."

The dining room is big enough for all of us to fit around the table. Platters are passed back and forth, and there's a lot of chatter and laughter.

It's as if we do this every week.

Maybe we did in another lifetime.

"You have a strange look on your face," Millie says across from me. "What's on your mind? Why aren't you two eating?"

"We already ate." I shrug a shoulder. "I have questions about these past lives."

Everyone around the table quiets and listens.

"You can ask anything," Lucien says. "I remember it all."

"That is an incredible burden to carry," I reply. "I was just thinking that we all fit together here as if we've done it many times. It's not awkward at all. No adjustments. So, I guess I was just curious if we've done this before."

Lucien swallows his food and purses his lips. "Well, in some lifetimes, we all lived together under one roof. It was the culture of the time. So, yes, we've done it before."

"Explains a lot," I say with a nod. "Also, is it horrible that I'm finding it hard to wrap my head around it?"

"Not horrible at all," Millie replies. "I'm still sorting it out, and I have *memories*. We're in an unusual situation."

"How is Oliver?" Miss Sophia asks.

"Oh, he looks so much better," Daphne says. "Like a whole new man. I was so relieved when we walked into his room and found him smiling, looking refreshed, and appearing at least ten years younger."

"Oh, that's so great," Brielle says.

"Who knew that being dehydrated could do so much damage?" Millie asks.

"Oh, there's Miss Annabelle now," Daphne says when her phone pings with a text. "She sent over the photo she took of you and Oliver at their house today. It's really a great picture. We'll have to frame it."

I glance down at it, nod, and then do a double-take.

"What's on him?" I ask.

"What do you mean?" Daphne says and looks closer. "It looks like shadows."

"There are no shadows on *me*." I take the phone from her and zoom in on the image. "Jesus. Oh, God."

"What is it?" Miss Sophia holds her hand out for the phone, and I pass it down.

Oliver is covered in handprints. His face, his arms. It looks like someone slapped him over and over again.

"What is that?" Brielle asks, looking over Miss Sophia's shoulder.

"I know," Ruth says quietly, her voice shaky. "I know exactly what that is. He's drawing his energy from Oliver. He's using him."

We all stare at each other in horror, and I immediately pick up the phone and call Oliver's number. But he doesn't pick up.

So, I call Miss Annabelle.

"Hello?" she says.

"Where's Oliver?"

"Oh, he went back to the restroom to take a shower. Do you need him?"

"Yes, ma'am. Please go get him. *Now*."

I can hear her walking through the house, opening a door.

"Ollie? Jack's on the phone for you. Oh, honey. What's wrong?"

"What is it?"

"He's on the floor. Breathing hard again. Oh, Jackson, something's wrong."

"Pack your bags," I say as I stand from the table. "You're coming to stay here. I'll be there in twenty minutes."

"Coming with you," Lucien says as he and Cash both hurry behind me.

"That son of a bitch," I growl as I roar my engine to life. "That motherfucking asshole. I'm going to make him pay for this."

CHAPTER SIXTEEN

Daphne

"How?" I demand once Oliver and Miss Annabelle are settled in their room. Miss Sophia and Mama are with them, helping to soothe exposed nerves. "How in the *hell* is this maniac able to get to Oliver, even with the protection spells and crystals in place?"

"He took the crystal down," Jack says and rubs his eyes. He's exhausted. "He said he took it down from above the mirror to cast another spell. It was just long enough for said maniac to make a move and get his hands on him."

"Poor Oliver," Brielle whispers. "He doesn't deserve this. He hasn't done *anything*."

"He loves me," Jack speaks up, catching all of our attention. "Daphne and I, we're the focus this time, right? Well, Oliver loves *me*, and that means Horace is fucking with him."

"Oliver and Annabelle are here now," Miss Sophia

says as she and Mama join us in the library. "And they're safe. I've covered the mirrors in their room just in case I missed anything, but I know I haven't. Horace can't get to anyone here in this house."

"Thank you," I say and reach out to take her hand. "Thank you so much for helping us."

"It's what I'm meant to do," she says simply. "What I was born for."

We blink in surprise and share glances.

"That's a big statement," Cash says.

"Isn't it, though?" Miss Sophia just smiles softly. "I'm here for you, for all of you, to help in any way I can. First, there's a spell I want you all to memorize. If he gets to you when you're not here, if he gets in your head, you can cast him out."

She begins to recite it, and Millie smiles at Lucien.

"That's the one we use," Millie says as Sanguine jumps into Millie's lap for some attention. "And it does work."

"Keep it in your toolbox," Miss Sophia instructs us. "It's powerful. Now, I think I'd like to go get some sleep."

"Goodnight, my sweet loves," Mama adds with a smile, and the two women leave the room.

"I need wine," I announce.

"Me, too," Brielle adds.

"That makes three of us," Millie says and sets her familiar down so she can walk to the antique bar in the corner that holds all of their alcohol and glasses.

"Lucien wanted to put this in the dining room or even the sitting room, but I wanted to have it handy in here since we spend so much time in the library."

"Good idea," Brielle says as Millie passes us each a glass of wine.

"While you three relax for a while—which you totally deserve—I'd like Cash and Jack to come with me." Lucien gestures for the guys to follow him.

Jackson leans over to kiss my cheek before he joins the others. Doing what, I have no idea.

Nor do I really care at this point.

I need an hour, just one measly hour of relaxation with my sisters.

"I'm tired," I admit with a sigh as I sip my wine. "Not in the normal, *oh, it's been a long workday* kind of tired. But the kind that settles deep in your bones when your *soul* is tired, you know?"

"Yeah," Brielle says and moves to sit next to me on the couch, taking my hand in hers. "I know. And it's pretty shitty."

"What if everything we've done up until now is wasted?" It's my worst nightmare, and it's a whisper. "You both worked so hard and defeated him twice. What if I screw this up for all of us this time?"

"Not possible," Millie says with way more confidence than I feel. "We're going to kick his sorry ass."

"Agreed." Brielle squeezes my hand. "Have you had any more dreams about Daddy?"

"Every night," I confirm. "Like clockwork. Though

it's not quite as scary since it was pointed out that it might not even *be* Daddy. It could just be *him* messing with me. Because aside from murder, that seems to be his favorite thing."

"I'll give you something for tonight," Millie says. "You'll sleep without dreams. Give your subconscious the night off."

"That sounds wonderful. Just don't put it in my wine."

"You can drink it as a tea just before bed," Millie says and then turns to Brielle. "I've been meaning to ask, do you still see the old lady shadow in our house?"

"Oh, yeah. She's not particularly thrilled that so many people are here. She just follows us all around like she's making sure no one steals the silver."

"You still haven't dropped your shields enough to see her?" I ask Millie.

"Nah. I don't need to. Brielle can see her. I'm just impressed that with as old as this house is, the old woman is our only ghost."

"Don't forget about the baby who cries," Brielle reminds her. "I hear her periodically. But I don't think that's an intelligent ghost—more of a residual echo is all. Aside from that, I don't see anything."

"Impressive," I agree. "And I can also say that when I touch things, the doorknobs and such, I don't pick up on anything bad. I only see happy memories. Families enjoying the house. Babies being born. That sort of thing."

"Can you see *us*?" Millie asks softly. "From before?"

I bite my lip because I've wondered how much to say about this since the first time I was here and Millie showed us the hiding place in the attic, where she found the box of treasures she'd hidden up there in her past life.

"I see all of it," I admit softly. "Bits and pieces of scenes in each room. Especially in your garden. I know that what's planted there now is new because Lucien added it after he rebought the house a few years ago, but you *loved* the gardens before. Spent a lot of time there."

"I did," Millie says with a nod.

"And you were so frustrated with Brielle and me," I say and smile when Brielle turns a surprised look at me.

"Us? Why us?"

"Because we didn't believe," I reply. "We didn't understand what was going on. Therefore, Millie and Lucien failed each time—and lost another lifetime."

"Well, that sucks," Brielle says. "I'm sorry."

"It's happening the way it's supposed to," Millie insists and refills our glasses.

Without even leaving her seat. No bottle needed apparently, as my glass is magically full again.

"I think you just like to show off your witchy skills," Brielle says, making our sister laugh.

I narrow my eyes on Millie as she sips her glass of merlot. "You got your hair done."

"Actually, I didn't. I just have a new tool. It's one of

those blow dryers with a brush thingie. And I have to tell you, it shaves lots of minutes off my hair time. And it looks like I went to the salon for a blowout."

"I think my curly hair would just get tangled in it," I say with a pout. "I like the highlights, too."

"Oh, I used the purple shampoo this morning," Millie says, brushing her fingers through her long, blonde hair as Brielle looks on, sipping her wine. "It was getting brassy, and I don't like brassy hair. I know that because my veins are blue. I'm supposed to look good in warm tones, but I like the cool tones better."

"What color would your veins be if they weren't blue?" I ask with a frown.

"Greenish. If your veins look green, you should wear cool tones," Millie informs us as we stare at our wrists, trying to figure out if our veins are blue or green.

"I'm sure it's not an exact science," I say philosophically. "So, if you like cool tones, go for it. I like it."

"Speaking of that," Brielle says, "Did you know that the perfect shade of lipstick for you is the same color as your nipples?"

We blink, stare at each other, and then all three of us lift our shirts to look down at our breasts.

That's how the guys find us seconds later.

"Are we interrupting something?" Cash asks lazily.

"Apparently," I say, not looking up at him, "my perfect shade of lipstick is the same shade as my nipples."

There's a stunned silence.

"I think you all need to stop drinking the wine," Jackson says at last.

"It's true," Brielle says. "I read it in *Cosmo*."

"Well, then, it's definitely true." Lucien scoops Millie up and plops her down on his lap. "Let's go to bed, my beloved."

"Will you check out my nipples for my perfect lipstick shade?"

"It's a burden I'm willing to carry."

———

"IT'S SO SLOW TODAY," I say with a frown. It's been a few days since we all settled into Millie and Lucien's house, and it's been quiet. Maybe too quiet. "I'm *never* this slow on a Saturday. It's just...weird. There's not even any traffic on the street."

"Maybe there's a festival or something going on that has everyone's interest," Jackson suggests.

"We're already past Mardi Gras," I remind him. "Ah, well, I guess we can use this time to rearrange some things. I need to dust and vacuum the rugs under the furniture. It'll be a catch-up day."

I turn to find my dust wand and glance up at the wall of mirrors, then gasp in horror.

"Oh, Goddess."

"Daph?"

"Oh, hell no. Just *go away*."

I'm backing up, but suddenly, Jackson is behind me, his strong arms wrapped around me.

"Talk to me, Daph. What do you see?"

"My father," I whisper. He's in every mirror, grinning at me in that horrible way he does, with those awful teeth. But he's different in every one. In some, he's laughing. In others, he's angry. "And none of them are the same. Shit, Jack."

"I got you," he says. "Remember the spell Miss Sophia told us to use last night?"

I nod, but I can't take my eyes off those mirrors.

"What if he comes through?" I ask. Every cell in my body is cold with fear. "What if he can get to me?"

"He can't," Jackson assures me. "He can't hurt you, Daphne. Say the spell with me."

"I-I-I don't remember it."

"Yes, you do. I'll start, and then you join me, okay?"

"Okay." I try to take a deep breath. "Okay."

"Lord and Lady, lend me your might.

Guardians of the watchtowers, make this right.

Ancestors and guides, hear my plea.

Toxic energy there will no longer be.

Evil and darkness be out of my life.

Leave my space with only light."

We recite the spell over and over again until, finally, he's gone from every mirror.

I spin in Jack's arms and cling to him, nauseous and overcome by fear.

"That's an image I never needed to have in my head."

"Hey, you're okay. I've got you."

"What if you weren't here?" I pull back, just far enough to look up into his face. "What would I have done?"

"You never have to know," he says simply. "Because I *am* here, and I'm not going anywhere. I think, for the time being, these mirrors should be covered."

"Yeah, I agree."

Suddenly, the nausea is back, so much worse than before, and I know.

I don't know how, I just do.

"Shit," I whisper and quickly move to the door.

But rather than a photograph on the stoop, there's a man.

A *body*.

Missing his eyes.

I stumble backward, screaming in terror.

I can hear Jackson speaking. Is he talking to me? No, he's on the phone.

I can't look away from the dead man on the doorstep.

"Get here. Fast."

He tosses his phone onto a nearby chair and yanks me to him.

"He was distracting us," I say into Jackson's chest. "So he could leave this here."

"I know." He strokes his hand down my hair. "I

know, baby. They're on their way. They'll be here in minutes. They were all at Witches Brew."

I nod and stare down at him. "I don't know him."

Someone slashed his throat. His mouth gapes open. And, like the Polaroids, he's missing his eyes.

My goddess, why the eyes? It's so damn fucking creepy.

Jack's right. The others arrive quickly, and I hear Cash speaking into his phone, already barking out orders.

"Gods," Lucien says and turns to Millie. "We need to cast a spell so passersby can't see this."

"Let's do it," Millie says, and I watch as they join hands and cast the circle. They're beautiful to watch together.

"What happened, exactly?" Cash asks.

We recount everything that happened over the past few minutes. "And then I opened the door and found him. I screamed a lot."

"I'm sure he took great pleasure in that," Millie says with a sigh. "And how, exactly, is he doing *this*?"

"He's stronger than ever before," Brielle says. "He's taking his victims' energy. He's growing stronger each day. And the eclipse is still a week away."

Suddenly, we're submerged in darkness. I can't see the others. I can't even hear them.

It's as though I'm alone in a pitch-black room.

"More parlor tricks?" I ask loudly. "More scare tactics?"

And then I remember. Recite the spell. If the others are doing it, too, then we can cast him out.

I take a deep breath and do my best to remember it all.

"Lord and Lady, lend me your might.

Guardians of the watchtowers, make this—"

I only get two lines in when the darkness disappears, and we're all standing in my shop, looking at each other.

"Wow, that spell *is* powerful," Brielle says. "We barely got any of it out before he was gone."

"Same," I say, nodding. "It worked."

"No." Lucien's voice and face are both grim as he shakes his head. "No, it didn't work. He's playing with us."

There's laughter all around us, and then the darkness descends again, even blacker than before.

I can't see the others. I can't even sense if they're nearby.

So, I start the spell once more.

"Lord and Lady, lend me your might.

Guardians of the watchtowers, make this right.

Ancestors and guides, hear my plea..."

Suddenly, I hear loud, maniacal laughter—as if he's heard the funniest joke of his life.

"Do you think that works on me?" he demands in a booming voice. "*Lord and Lady, lend me your might.*"

He's mocking, using a high-pitched singsong voice.

"You're pathetic. I could simply kill you where you

stand. And I should. Because you've defied me at every turn."

Oh, Goddess, I'm drowning. I can't catch my breath. I can't get to the surface of the water. I thrash about, searching for relief.

And just when the edges of my mind go dark, I'm free.

I fall and struggle for breath, gasping. I blink at the bright light coming in through the windows.

"Are you okay?" Jackson asks as he hurries to gather me up. "Daphne, are you okay?"

"He was drowning me," I say at last.

"I was on fire," Brielle adds. "It felt like someone set me on fire."

"Hanging," Millie says, rubbing her neck. "I was hanging from a noose."

Lucien swears and pulls his wife close. We're all embracing, trying to regroup.

"I was being stabbed, over and over again," Jackson says.

"I had my throat slit," Cash adds.

Everyone turns their eyes to Lucien.

"Stoned." He clears his throat. "I was being stoned to death. Crushed."

"What in the hell?" I demand.

"It's how we've all died in the past," Lucien explains. "In different lifetimes, we died that way. I don't understand how he knows that, but he's showing it to us."

"A threat?" Cash asks. "A way of saying: '*If you don't do what I want, I'll just do this to you again.*'"

"Maybe," Millie says.

"How did it stop?" I ask. "What made it all stop and drive him away?"

"It could be that he ran out of energy," Jackson suggests. "But one thing is very clear. The protection spells and crystals don't work this time. He's too strong. And even though we're formidable when we're together, it's not enough."

"I won't lose," I say, shaking my head. "I will *not* let him win this time."

"We have one week to get ready," Lucien says. "We need to study, and we need to be with others who may know more than we do."

"Looks like an impromptu witches' conference is about to hit New Orleans," Brielle says. "Because that's the best idea I've heard in a long time."

"I'm scared." It's a whispered admission in the dark as Jack and I lie in bed. We spent the day telling the story of what happened this morning over and over again, trying to pick it apart and figure out what the next moves are. "And I'm not alone. I saw the fear in Miss Sophia's eyes today, and she's *never* scared, Jack."

"She's worried."

"She's *afraid*. You can't deny it."

"I think we're all uneasy about this," he says and rolls me onto my back so he can look down at me. He brushes my hair off my cheek. "It makes sense that this third round is the most difficult. That he would escalate like this. It sucks, and it's not fair, but I don't think anything about this is exactly *fair*."

"No. It's not." I lightly brush my fingertip over his Adam's apple.

"You're formidable, Daphne. You're smart, you have a gift, and you have it in you to defeat this monster. You *do*," he insists when I start to shake my head. "You just need your confidence. Stop second-guessing yourself. Stop letting him *scare* you."

"If you're not scared, you're not human," I insist.

"I'm just saying. You're the boss here. *You* are. Not him. The next time he shows you your father, kick some ass. The next time he tries to bully you, kick him in the balls."

"There's a lot of violence in this pep talk," I say but smile and kiss his chin. "I get it. Stop cowering and stand up for myself. Stop giving in to the bully."

"Yeah. Exactly. We can do this. And we're about to gather all the tools and weapons we need to win not only the battle but also the war."

"I guess we'd better get some sleep then, huh?"

He kisses me softly. "We have a little time."

And in the dark, he reminds me of who we are together.

CHAPTER SEVENTEEN

"I saw the light over the confessional, and the voice said: That's the person to kill."
-Herbert Mullin

"If you want something done right," he says as he stalks around the living room in the body he's inhabited, his hands fisting, his breath coming fast, "you have to do it your damn self."

He's been using this one anyway. As an errand runner, mostly. He hasn't used him for energy because he needs this toy to be strong.

How else can he deliver corpse gifts to his Daphne? The photos?

Yes, this toy has done well. He's a *man*, much

stronger than that little bitch he used before. And the link he has to the girls isn't lost on Horace.

It only makes it that much more fun.

He walks to the mirror in the dirty bathroom and grins at himself.

Yes, he recognizes the face.

And so will the girls when the time is right.

"We have much to do," he says to his reflection. "We have to punish them first. They're so *obstinate* right now. But, I suppose, kids will be kids. Still, we need to show them discipline, and punishment is part of that."

Now that he has a body again, he'll be able to *feel* the work with his hands. The thought fills him with impatience and the need to get started right away.

It's going to be a delight—an absolute joy.

A smile spreads over his face.

"Yes, we have much to do. First, we need some supplies. As excited as I am to get started, you just don't have the facilities I need. But not to worry. We can fix that easily enough. It won't take long.

"Now, the first thing we need is a workbench. And a very sharp knife."

THEY'RE mewling behind him in that way the toys always do when they're afraid. He'd missed that— almost as much as he missed using the knife on the toys.

"Girls," he says as he turns to them. He can't help but smile. The remaining four are just so *beautiful*. "You must calm down now. I know, you're excited. I am, too. But we can't rush. I admit I went a little too fast with those first two. But, oh, it just felt so wonderful to get back to work. Now, shush. Just relax. You've only been here for one day."

He smiles kindly. There are two redheads, and they were hard to find. It's true that gingers are scarce in the population, so he had to hunt a bit for these two. And now, they're too precious to waste. He'll hold them for a while.

The other two, one blonde and the other brunette, sit huddled together. They're *real* sisters, which only makes him even more elated.

"Yes, this is exactly as it should be." He turns from them and whistles for a moment as he lays his freshly cleaned tools on the brand-new workbench. "It was fun to play through the mirrors, but this is so much more efficient. Especially given how much you've disappointed me lately."

He turns and frowns at the girls.

"Don't worry. You'll receive your punishments. Then, all will be well. Millie." He turns with a bright smile. "Let's have a little fun, shall we?"

CHAPTER EIGHTEEN

Jackson

"We're fighting an evil spirit, not vampires," Daphne says to Millie, who's currently coating bread with butter and garlic to go into the oven. "That's a lot of garlic, Mill."

"And it's good for you," Millie replies, adds just a touch more garlic out of principle, and then slides the pan into the oven. "Besides, it wards off evil, and it's hard to use in spells, so I'm feeding it to you."

"Oh, good. Give me extra garlic." I wink at Millie as I carry the dishes and silverware into the dining room so I can set the table for dinner. I didn't grow up with a big family, but I always had a lot of people around when I was in the Army, so prepping for big meals hasn't been that big of an adjustment.

Brielle follows me with napkins.

"Cash is on his way here from the station," she says. "He got called in this morning, even though his boss gave him the okay to take a couple of weeks of personal time. He wouldn't tell me what was so important, and I know we're not supposed to go anywhere alone, but it's been so quiet for a few days."

"I don't trust it," Daphne says as she joins us, carrying a steaming pot of pasta. "It's been *too* quiet. How do we go from constant onslaught of awful to just *nothing*?"

"Maybe he's playing with us again," Millie suggests and smiles at Lucien, who joins us, as well. He's been in his home office all day. "Anything?"

"No."

We have close to a hundred witches planning to come to New Orleans to help us during the eclipse in just a few days.

In the meantime, he's spent many hours on video calls with many other highly experienced witches, trying to come up with the best plan for the eclipse.

He looks damn tired, and I feel guilty. He's already fought his fight. This one is on Daphne and me. I feel like I should be doing *more*.

"Where are the others?" Daphne asks as she looks around the table. "Is it just the six of us for dinner tonight?"

"Mama, Miss Sophia, Oliver, and Miss Annabelle had dinner in the garden earlier," Millie says. "And they went for a long walk. Said they needed to get out for a bit."

"Cash said to get started eating without him,"

Brielle says as she dishes up her plate with spaghetti and bread. "He's in traffic. He'll eat when he gets here."

"It'll be hot for him," Millie says as we settle in to eat dinner.

"I don't trust how quiet it's been," I say, at last, breaking the silence and picking up the conversation from earlier. "It's been three days with *nothing*. We're going to work, living our lives, and it's as if everything is just normal."

"And you're complaining?" Brielle asks. "I say enjoy the break while we have it because I'm pretty sure when he decides to start in again, it won't be simple. And it won't be easy."

"I don't like it, either," Millie says. "I keep looking over my shoulder, jumping at the littlest things. I'm waiting for the other shoe to drop."

"It's another mind game," Lucien says. "And that's what he's been doing this whole time, right? Playing with our heads? Well, this time, after he scared the hell out of everyone, he stops and lets us get comfortable and confident again before starting back in for another round."

"I know I say this a lot," I chime in, "but he's a sick son of a bitch."

"Well, yeah," Millie says. "Of course, he is. I guess there's nothing we can do. Just go about our business unless something happens."

The frustration is powerful. And constant. I hate

that Daphne is always afraid. That she questions herself. I want this over for her.

For all of us.

"I know it's a lot of garlic," Brielle says as she takes a bite of bread, "but man, it's good."

Headlights cast a glow through the room, and Brielle grins.

"Cash is home."

"Is it dark out already?" Daphne says with a frown. "And the others are still out walking?"

"They're fine," I assure her. "Four witches together, especially *those* four, is formidable."

"You're right."

Our heads come up when Cash walks into the dining room, his computer gripped under one arm.

His expression looks grim.

His eyes search for Brielle and then soften when he finds her.

"What's wrong?" she asks her husband. "Why did they call you in today?"

"We have six new missing persons cases. All women between the ages of twenty-five and thirty."

His mouth firms into a hard line as he opens his computer, taps some keys, and then turns the screen so we can all see.

The air seems to leave the room.

Millie gasps.

Brielle hangs her head in her hands.

Looking out at us from the screen are six women. Two redheads, three blondes, and one brunette.

"She looks familiar," Millie says and points to one of the redheads.

"Of course, she does," Cash replies. "She looks like Daphne. They *all* look familiar."

"He's back to this now?" Daphne demands and stands to pace the room. "He's back to kidnapping and torturing girls?"

"We don't know that he's torturing them," I say, but the woman I love whirls on me with fire in her eyes.

"That's what he does," she says. "He hurts and kills people, Jack."

"I know. I was trying to stay positive."

"My goddess," Millie says softly. "He just keeps changing the game."

"We knew things were changing when we found that corpse in front of Daphne's doorway," I remind everyone. "And the one thing this asshole is consistent about is being inconsistent. He is playing with us."

Brielle stands and joins Daphne at the window. Both sisters have their arms folded across their chests and are staring out at the street.

"Oh, God." Brielle's voice is suddenly shaking and full of fear.

"What is it?" Cash asks and hurries to her.

"You don't see them, do you?" Brielle points outside. We all join her, but I don't see anything but a sidewalk. "The girls."

"Oh, B," Millie says and brushes her hand down her sister's hair. "How many?"

"Two." Brielle turns back to the open computer on the table. "I can't be one hundred percent certain because they're missing their eyes, but I think it's these two."

She gestures to one blonde and the brunette.

"I recognize the scar on the chin of this one, and the hair on the blonde."

Cash wraps her up in a big hug, his face full of anger and fear. "Is that it? Just the eyes are gone?"

She shakes her head and takes a long, deep breath. "No. One was hanged. The noose is still around her neck. And the other... Well, let's just say he *really* has a thing for disemboweling."

"Jesus," I mutter and wipe my hand over my face. "Is this what happened before?"

"Yes." Brielle's eyes meet mine. "But something is different now. There's something new."

"What? What's different?" Daphne demands.

"He carved *Bad Girl* into their flesh. He's punishing us."

"Hell." Millie sits and scrubs her hands over her face. "He took three days off to shift gears. To somehow kill these girls."

"Wait," Daphne says with her hand up. "I didn't receive a photo of these kills. I received Polaroids for all the others—well, besides the poor man on my doorstep. Cash, did you ever find out who he is?"

"Yeah." The other man sighs and pulls his hand down his face. "His name is Matthew Guthrie. *Was*. He lived in the bayou. Recluse, loner. In his sixties."

"He used to be a part of the dark coven," Lucien says quietly. "I never met him. Only heard the name. He left the coven years ago from what I heard."

"How are we supposed to catch him when he's so all over the place?" Daphne asks.

"We're not supposed to catch him," I remind her. "We're going to defeat him. On the night of the eclipse."

"He's right," Lucien agrees. "We can't catch him. But we *can* end him. I have a few things left to delve into, but I think I'm close to figuring this out."

"Why so much research?" I ask.

"Because we've never gotten this far before," he replies. "We've never been this close to defeating him. Which could also explain his erratic behavior. He doesn't know how to handle it either."

"Wait." Daphne holds up a hand and shakes her head. "Does Horace *know* that we've done this throughout many lifetimes?"

Lucien frowns, but before he can speak, she continues.

"I know that he tried to hurt us in ways that we've all overcome before, but I'm not convinced that he's aware this has been going on for as long as it has. Maybe he's just reborn every time, full of so much evil and hate, and it's a constant loop."

"Either way, it's fucked-up," Cash points out, and I can't help but smile.

"Oh, I'm not suggesting that anyone feel sorry for him," Daphne agrees. "I just don't know if he realizes the significance of it all. Is he that smart?"

"Since we don't know, *can't* know what he understands," Millie says slowly, thinking it over, "we'll proceed as if he *does* know. Because at the end of the day, whether or not he knows changes nothing."

"You're right," Daphne says, her shoulders slumping. "You're totally right."

"TONIGHT IS ABOUT *US*," I announce the following day as we lock up the shop for the evening.

Daphne turns to me in surprise.

"How are we going to manage that? We're currently living in a house full of people."

I take her hand and link our fingers, kissing her knuckles.

"We're not headed that way for a while yet," I inform her. "We're going out for dinner and then for a walk in Audubon Park. I want to be with you, just you, for a little while. I don't mind staying with the others. I know it's important, and I *like* them. But I just got you back in my life, and I want some time with you. What do you say?"

She grins, her eyes filling with excitement.

"I say let's do it. Where are we going for dinner?"

Rather than getting in my car, I walk her down the street to a little restaurant nestled back in a courtyard with old cobblestones for a floor, exposed brick walls, and some of the best jambalaya I've ever had in my life.

When we're shown to our table, Daphne smiles and glances around, then turns to me and sips her water.

"What is it?"

She raises a brow.

"What do you see? I can always tell when you see something you enjoy. You get that sweet smile on your face."

"This used to be a hospital," she says. "And, normally, that wouldn't be a fun thing to see, but so many babies were born here. There was a lot of joy. A few sad moments, of course, but lots of love."

The waitress comes to take our order, and then I lean in and take Daph's hand. It's nice to be away from the others and have a meal as if we're a normal couple out on a date.

But the edges of my vision start to gray. I swear under my breath, but I can't stop the premonition from coming.

"Why are you doing this?"

I'm in a room with the women from Cash's computer. Well, three of them. Another is gone.

"Because, Daphne, you've been a bad girl, and I have to punish you and your sisters." His voice is perfectly calm. Pleasant, even. "I know you don't mean to be bad. I know that you're

nothing but a woman, and it's clear to me that those men you've chosen to lie with haven't done a good job of reminding you that men are the bosses. You're supposed to do what we say, Daphne. You're supposed to bend to our will."

"I'll do whatever you say," the woman says, her voice tinged with fear and desperation. "I'll do everything you say. I have no problem with that."

"You're lying." He turns to her and smiles. "I know you're lying. You're just saying what I want to hear—though I appreciate you trying to be flexible."

He walks to her and slaps her across the face.

"But you're a filthy liar, and that's just one more thing to punish you for. Maybe before I take your eyes, I'll take that pretty little tongue."

"Jack?"

I shake my head and look into Daphne's worried eyes.

"What was it?"

The waitress saves me by delivering our meals. After seeing what I just did, I'm not super hungry, but I also don't want to ruin our evening.

When our plates sit before us, I force a smile at Daphne. "This looks good."

"You're evading."

"I don't know what you're talking about." I take a bite of my food and then gesture to hers with my fork. "Better dig in, or I'll steal it."

She smirks but eats her meal, and the conversation

shifts to movies we've seen lately and what shows we like to stream.

"I *love* the show *Lucifer*," she says with a grin. "The guy who plays the devil is one hot man."

I stop chewing and frown at her. "Hey."

"What?"

"I'm sitting right here."

"So?"

"So why are you talking about hot men?"

She laughs and sips her water. "Please. It's not like you don't find female celebrities attractive."

"I'm not talking about them with you," I point out. "Out of courtesy."

"Do you think you'll eventually have a hot-and-heavy affair with Sandra Bullock?"

I mean, I probably wouldn't if she offered.

Probably.

She sits back, finished with her meal, and grins at me. "You're fun. You know that?"

"Hell, yes, I'm a good time." I chuckle and pay the waitress. "Are you ready for more fun?"

"Absolutely. I need to walk off this food."

I take her hand as we leave the restaurant and walk down to my car. The drive to Audubon Park takes a little while, thanks to traffic, but we don't care.

We're just enjoying our quiet time together.

After I find a place to park, Daphne and I set off on a walk through the ancient oak trees, their limbs so big and heavy they rest on the ground. Other people mill about, running and riding bikes, having picnics, tossing balls.

It's a busy place, but I like it.

"Dinner was good," Daph says and swings our hands back and forth as we walk along the paved path. "Thanks."

"You're welcome."

"So, are you going to tell me what you saw?"

I sigh and glance her way. She watches me with patient eyes.

"I'm getting really sick and tired of this asshole ruining my time with you."

She just waits. Finally, I guide her to a bench and we take a seat.

"I was with him. Wherever he is. And I saw the girls."

Daphne's eyes round, and she holds my hand tightly.

"I'm sorry, Jack."

"The frustrating part is, I don't know that I can pin down where I was. It's just a room. No windows. I couldn't see outside. I have no idea where he's holding them in the city. If he's even *in* the city."

"Cash might be able to ask the right questions to get more information," she suggests. She fidgets in her seat and then stands. "Let's keep walking."

"What's wrong with the bench?"

"Someone slept on it last night who was thinking about throwing himself into the Mississippi River. It's not a happy place to sit."

We're quiet for a long moment, just breathing in the fresh air around us. It's still winter, so it's not too hot yet.

The night is a breezy eighty degrees.

"Do you still like to run?" she asks out of the blue. "For exercise?"

"Not really. I ran too much in the Army. Took the fun out of it for me. Why, do *you* run?"

"Only if something's chasing me."

I pull her closer, wrap my arm around her, and kiss her temple. "You make me laugh."

After an hour of walking around, we make our way back to my car and then toward Millie and Lucien's place.

"It was nice to steal this time away," she says and reaches over to rest her hand on my thigh. "Thanks for it."

"Anytime."

We walk up to the front porch, and Daphne pauses, holding onto her stomach.

"What's wrong?"

"I wonder if I ate something bad." She scowls, and then her eyes clear. "No. Oh, shit."

She hurries around me, and I follow after her.

Sitting on the doormat is an envelope.

We both sigh in frustration.

"What's that holding it down?"

"A bloodstone."

CHAPTER NINETEEN

Daphne

Of course, this would happen now after a fun evening with Jack. I can't seem to catch a break lately.

I walk around the envelope on the doorstep, open the front door, and call out for my sisters.

"Guys? Brielle? Millie?"

"We're in the library," Millie calls back.

"I need you out here." Jack's still on the porch, his hands on his hips, and his face set in grim lines. I want to run into his arms. I want to pull him away and go anywhere but here. Somewhere it's only the two of us and we don't have to deal with all of this mess. But I can't.

"Is Cash here?"

"I'm here," Cash says as all four hurry from the library. He sighs when he sees where I'm pointing. "Did you touch it?"

"No, we haven't touched anything."

"There's a bloodstone," Millie says and reaches for Lucien.

"He's back to taunting all of us," Brielle says, her eyes trained on the sidewalk. "I see a third girl."

"It's creepy, and a blessing that the girls can't come inside," Millie says.

Cash passes out gloves to all of us.

"Do you just carry dozens of these around in your pocket?" I ask as I slide my hand inside.

"These days, I do. I know there won't be any prints, but I'm a cop. We do this by the book."

I kind of love that he's so strict.

Once his gloves are on, Cash retrieves the stone and the envelope, and we all file back into the library.

Millie moves to close the blinds on the windows. "I don't want those girls looking in here. And I don't want Brielle to have to see them, either."

Cash sets the bloodstone and envelope on the table before us, and we're all quiet as we look at them, each lost in our own thoughts—and so damn angry that this is happening.

"I guess we have to get this over with." I pick up the envelope and frown. "I don't feel a heartbeat on this one. Or any heat."

I look up at Jackson, whose eyes have narrowed.

I glance at Cash.

"I have to take off the gloves. Sorry, Cash."

I pull them off, toss them aside, and pick up the envelope once more.

Suddenly, not only can I feel the heartbeat and the heat, but I can also see.

Everything.

"Oh, Goddess."

"What?" Lucien sits forward. "What is it?"

"I'm not blocked anymore." I swallow hard and feel so many emotions swamping me that it brings tears to my eyes. "Oh, shit. Shit, shit, shit."

"Okay, set it down." Miss Sophia, who's just come into the room, moves quickly to me, taking my hand. "Set that down and focus, Daphne. I want you to breathe."

Mama comes in as well and sits between Millie and Brielle. Her eyes are full of concern and worry. She fiddles with the mother of pearl pendant that hangs from her neck.

And that reminds me to touch mine. My rose quartz is smooth, cool to the touch, and bolsters my confidence. I take a long, deep breath. My spirit calms just a bit.

"I wasn't ready for that," I admit. "Why isn't he still blocking me?"

"Because he knows this is almost over," Miss Sophia says calmly. "And he wants to gloat."

I clear my throat, take one more breath, and then pick up the envelope.

"What do you see, Daphne?" Miss Sophia's voice is as calm as a lake in the early morning. "I want you to tell us what you see. Set yourself apart from it. It's not personal."

"Yeah, right." I clear my throat and lick my lips. "Okay, I'm in a house. Someone's home, anyway. It's kind of dirty. And it's like I'm looking through his eyes."

I hear the tremor in my voice and straighten my spine.

"Is that normal for you?" Lucien asks. "To see things through someone's eyes?"

"Sometimes. Usually, I just feel the emotions and catch snippets of things that have happened."

"Keep going," Miss Sophia urges. "What's happening in the house?"

I want to whimper from the intense hate and pure evil that permeates the dwelling. I lift my shields even more so I don't absorb the emotions.

"He's having fun. He likes the punishments, and he's excited that he gets to do it with his own hands again, rather than making them do it to themselves. It's not as satisfying to him if he's not the one doing it. Physically."

I swallow and let more sensations come to me.

"He loves us." My eyes snap open, and I feel the need to throw up, so I rush down the hall to a bathroom and barely make it to the toilet. Someone holds my hair back and coos at me, but all I hear is the rushing in my ears. All I feel is the need to get everything I just saw and felt out of me.

"It's okay," Jackson croons as he rubs a circle over my back. "I'm here, sweets. I'm right here."

I lean my head on my arm and try to catch my breath, then sit back on my haunches and accept the wet rag from Jack, wiping my face.

"I'm okay," I say at last. "It just slammed into me. And it's slimy."

"You don't have to explain yourself." He helps me to my feet and pulls me in for a hug. "I love you, Daphne. It's going to be okay."

I let myself cling to him for just a minute, soaking up his strength. For the first time in a long while, I *read* him the way I used to be able to.

Love.

Concern.

Anger—but not at me.

"I love you, too. Thanks. Let me just rinse my mouth, and then I think we can go back in."

He never lets go of my hand as we walk back to the library. Everyone is sitting, just as they were before, but I can read the worry on their faces.

"I'm okay." I accept the water Millie offers and take a long drink, then sit back in my seat beside Miss Sophia.

And reach for the envelope.

"He loves us," I say again and wrinkle my nose in disgust. "He believes he does, anyway. He's teaching us lessons, punishing us. He's angry but also resigned. Like he knows that women just misbehave this way and need his punishments."

"Where is he?" Cash asks. "Where is he keeping the girls?"

"I don't know." And that has me feeling the sickest of all. "I can't see much. I can't see how he gets to wherever he is. He's moving through the house. I don't see any of the girls. He's cleaning because he's disgusted by how dirty the place is.

"He's walking down the hall into a bathroom, and—" I frown in confusion. "He's looking at himself in the mirror. Oh, shit. For fuck's sake." I open my eyes and stand, shaking my head. "No. He's dead. I *know* he's dead."

"What?" Brielle takes my hands in hers and makes me look into her eyes. "What is it? What do you see, Daph?"

"He has Daddy's face." I shake my head again in denial. "It's impossible. Is he just messing with me again? He has to be. He can't be using our father to kill these girls."

I turn to Mama, desperate for answers.

"He's dead." I hear the plea in my voice. "You killed him. I know you did."

"I didn't," she says, shaking her head. "But the *thing* that inhabited me did, yes. And then he proceeded to torment you girls, and me, for the better part of twenty years."

"Then how?"

"I'm not finished," Mama says, her voice stern. "Your father had a brother. Andy."

"How did we not know that?" Brielle asks the room at large.

"Your father told me, back when Brielle was just a baby, that he killed Andy. Because Andy said something, in passing, about me being pretty."

"Temper much?" Cash asks.

"I've never seen a man more filled with rage," Mama says with a sigh. "When we met, he was *not* like that. He was quick to smile, always made me laugh, and was kind. He didn't love that I was part of the coven. But I wasn't willing to give that up, and he said he could live with it. But right after Brielle was born, things started to change. He was just angry all the time. Horrible. He would say the meanest things."

"You're remembering more," I say, shocked at how much she knows. I know she's been doing so much better, but there are moments I'm surprised by the difference in her.

"Much more. At least from before the possession. I admit, having a grumpy husband, I was moody, as well. It's exhausting, always walking on eggshells.

"Brielle couldn't have been six months old when he came home one night, soaked to the skin because of a big storm. That was the night he told me he had killed Andy. I was shocked. I knew he had been in a bad mood, but I had no idea he was homicidal. It terrified me. And then, the next day, he just...changed. Suddenly, he was the same happy man I married, and things calmed down for a while. I had two more babies and thought maybe things would be different.

"But then Daphne was about a year old or so, and it got horrible again. He was just so mean. So awful. And I only wanted to keep you girls safe. I didn't want him to hurt you. He'd tell me he was fixin' to hit me. Slap me around. Teach me a lesson.

"And he did. Way too often."

I reach over and take her hand, giving it a squeeze. "I'm so sorry, Mama."

"It wasn't your fault. It was his. Things start to get fuzzy after that. Whatever lurked in that house started to play with my mind, too. And then I wasn't myself for a long, long time."

"So, Adam *said* he killed Andy," Cash says, "but we don't have any proof of that. You never confirmed it?"

"I—no. I didn't. He never came around no more." Mama frowns. "Do you think maybe he lied to me?"

"Were Adam and Andy twins?" Lucien asks.

"Yes, I think so. I didn't know Adam's family all that well. His parents both died when he was a boy, and his grandmama raised him and his brother. She died before we got married. He didn't have much other family to speak of."

"So, maybe I wasn't seeing Daddy," I say, thinking it over. "But his brother."

"Did he look younger or older in your mind?" Miss Sophia asks.

"I guess he was older," I reply as I think it over. "More wrinkles and some gray hair. But the same eyes."

Cash taps on his computer. "Andy Landry, lives in Baton Rouge. I have an address. I'm calling the local authorities and will head up that way."

"Clearly, we're all coming with you."

"I'm not," Mama says, shaking her head.

"Ruth and I will stay here," Miss Sophia says. "Oliver and Annabelle are due home soon. We'll fill them in. Please, keep us posted."

"We will."

"It can't be this easy," Jackson whispers to me as we hurry to his car. We'll follow behind the others filing into Cash's car.

"Maybe it can. We could use a leg up on this jerk."

Jack shakes his head. "I don't buy it."

"NOTHING," Cash says as he walks over to us. We all stood on the sidewalk, waiting as Cash joined the local authorities to look through the little rundown house. "There's nothing in there. Looks like Andy hasn't been home in a while. Horace isn't using this place as his fucking torture lair."

"He could be literally *anywhere*," I say as my stomach falls. "How will we find him? How will we find those women? Goddess only knows what he's doing to them right now."

"I think it's time for a little blood magic," Millie says, looking right at Jackson. "We know someone who can help with that."

"No. No way," Jack says, shaking his head emphatically. "We're not getting them involved. They've been through enough."

And then, as he speaks, his expression goes lax, and his eyes cloud over.

"He's having a premonition," I say softly, linking my hand with his and letting him know he's not alone.

"Can you see what he does?" Brielle asks. "When you touch him?"

"No. We're not linked that way. But he can feel me."

Brielle keeps looking down the street, frowning, and then away.

"What is it?" I ask her.

"There are four." She closes her eyes. "And their deaths were awful."

Cash pulls her against him, not caring at all that the cops currently leaving the house and getting into their vehicles give him funny looks.

"They think I'm crazy," he says with a sigh. "And, honestly, I don't care. If it meant possibly finding those girls here, it was worth it."

Suddenly, Jackson blinks and frowns.

"I know where he is," he says and wipes his free hand over his eyes. "We need to get to the bayou."

"Do you have an address?" Cash asks.

"No," Lucien says, narrowing his eyes as he watches Jackson. "He doesn't need one."

Jack shakes his head and looks down at me. "My parents' house."

"Didn't you sell it?" I ask with a frown. "Someone must live in it."

"I sold it. No idea what was done with it after. I'm telling you, he's in that house. I recognized the kitchen."

"Let's go," Cash says. "You're in the lead, Jack. I'll follow you."

We hurry to the cars, and when Jackson pulls away from Andy's house, he swears under his breath.

"It makes sense," he says. "Of course, he'd target that place. I'm linked to it, and it has the bad energy from my dad killing himself."

"Jack." I rub his arm and feel the tension roll off him in waves. "What was happening? In the vision."

"He was cleaning his tools in the sink. Blood everywhere. He was fucking *whistling* as if he were doing the dinner dishes. Then, a scream came from somewhere in the house, and the fucker smiled. Like it made him so damn happy. He grabbed his power drill, put a bit in it, and walked out of the kitchen.

"I didn't follow him. I pulled myself out of the vision. I know it's chickenshit of me—"

"No, it's not," I insist. "No one wants to see that, Jack."

"I figured I know where he is. We can just go get

him. And, hopefully, save the girls before he drills holes in them."

He glances at me, his face filled with torment.

"I've seen war, Daph. I've seen, firsthand, what men can do to each other. I've watched soldiers be blown apart, shot, you name it. But I've never seen anything like this."

"Of course, not. There's never *been* anyone like this."

He's quiet for the rest of the drive. I could find his old house with my eyes closed; I spent so much of my time there when I was young.

Jackson pulls to a stop in the driveway, and both of our jaws drop.

"No one's here," I say quietly. "Nobody's been here for a long, long time."

"Why would someone buy it if they didn't want to live in it?" Jack asks. "It doesn't make any sense."

"I don't know." I glance up to find Millie standing next to my door. I step out of the car and look at the others. "There's no one here."

"I know," Millie says. "I reached out to see. I know." She holds up a hand before I can scold her for dropping her shields. "But lives are at stake here, and I needed to know. There's nothing living in that house."

"You'll want to go inside," Lucien says to Jack, who just nods. "We'll go with you. Cash and I will go."

Brielle joins Millie and me as the three men step up to the door. Lucien flicks his hand, and the door unlocks and opens.

"It's so cool that you guys can do that," I whisper to my sister. She turns back to me with a smile.

"Lucien just gets sexier every day." She sighs in happiness. "And you should see what he can do with fire."

"I've seen," I remind her. "And it's impressive."

"You should see what Cash can do with handcuffs." Brielle's smile is as bright as the sun. "It's magical in its own way."

"Hell, yes," I say with a laugh. "I'm sure it is."

A few minutes later, the guys come back outside. Jack's face is set in angry lines.

"What's in there?" I ask.

"Nothing," he says. "Literally, *nothing*. Whoever bought it hasn't stepped foot inside since the day it sold."

"Odd," Lucien says quietly. "But I guess people can be odd. It's not against the law."

"Something doesn't feel right," Millie says slowly. "Like it's all more smoke and mirrors."

"Well, I can tell you that there's nothing inside," Cash says. "Except about three inches of dust and maybe a mouse or two. The structure is surprisingly sound for sitting empty in the bayou for so many years."

"That's just it," Lucien says. "After just a couple of years, it should have started to decay. It wasn't a new house when Jack sold it."

"No, it was a good fifty years old then," Jackson agrees. "But no one's inside."

"Now what?" I ask, suddenly exhausted. "He's just got us on a wild goose chase."

"He's distracting us," Brielle says. "Keeping us from the most important thing, and that's coming up with a plan to get rid of him. Instead, he has us running all over Louisiana."

"You're right." Jackson takes one last look at the house. "Let's go back to Millie and Lucien's and regroup."

We turn back to the cars. I swear I see a curtain move out of the corner of my eye, but when I look up at the house, it's still.

CHAPTER TWENTY

"I killed so many women, I have a hard time keeping them straight."
-Gary Holmes, The Green River Killer

"Why do you continue to underestimate me?" He paces the room, his footfalls heavy, his hands fisted in anger. He's never been so angry in his life.

Even on the day he killed his mother, he wasn't this angry.

"You think you can just *come here* and stop what I've started?" He turns and glares at his toys. They're all weeping, especially the newest one he took early this morning—naked and crying on the little mattresses he laid on the floor for them. "I've given you every chance, girls. Every chance there is to show me that you're worthy of everything I've done for you. And I've done plenty. You know. You saw it all."

He shakes his head in disgust and rubs his hand over his sweaty face.

"I spent *years* making everything good for you. Just perfect. I've taken blood. Eyes. I've sent the ghosts to you so you could see. So you could get excited. So you would WORSHIP ME!"

His face turns red as he yells in their faces.

"But you're ungrateful! Just like all the other women I've known. You're ungrateful."

He smiles then, seemingly calm.

"And that just won't do, ladies."

He paces slower now in front of the girls, his hands linked behind his back as if he's a sergeant looking over his troops.

"You're not who I thought you were. I've denied it for a while because I wanted to believe in you. To see the best in you. But I was wrong. You're not wonderful. You're not for me. And because of that, you have to pay."

He turns to his toys and clucks his tongue.

"Now, now. There's no need to carry on so dramatically. These hysterics are getting old, to be honest. How are those burns coming along?"

He leans in to check on a blonde woman who's covered in tiny burns from her neck to her toes.

"Healing. That's good. Probably hurts, doesn't it?"

She presses her lips together and lets out a low moan of despair.

"ANSWER ME!"

"Y-y-yes. Yes, it hurts."

"Good. See now? We just have to be kind to each other. Even though our time together grows shorter, we have to be kind. There's no need to be otherwise."

He licks his lips, pondering which method to use on each of the remaining toys.

"Of course, now that I've decided you're not the girls I want, the ones I *need*, we'll have to speed this along a bit. I have so much to do. You understand, of course."

He reaches for the girl with the burns, and she begins silently weeping, the tears flowing like little rivers from her eyes.

"Please," she murmurs. "Please, just let me go."

"Now, Millie. You know that's not how this works. When will you learn? Oh, that's right. You won't. You just won't learn. So, you have to die."

The other toys gasp, cry, even scream as they watch Horace slowly burn the flesh from his toy until the life finally leaves her eyes.

And then he turns to the next.

The temper, the tempo increases as he makes his way through them, slicing and cutting, stabbing, drilling. It's a fevered frenzy of murder, one full of rage and blood and absolute horror. Until he turns to the remaining plaything.

The other toys' sprayed blood matts her red hair, though her face is dirty and dry.

No tears on this one.

He grins, his chest heaving from the exertion of his work.

"You're the only one left, Daphne."

And without another word, he simply swings out his hand and slits her pretty, white throat from ear to ear.

When she falls to the floor, he smiles in satisfaction.

"There, now. I'll have to finish this, of course. But first..."

He walks to a bathroom and stares at the face of the man he took—the one who's done his bidding for quite a while now.

"I don't need you anymore, Andy. Just like I didn't need your brother. You were both disappointments. Did you think I wouldn't find you?"

A single tear slips out of his eye. He can feel Andy fighting him.

And that won't do.

"Goodbye, Andy."

He takes the knife and stabs his eyes out.

CHAPTER TWENTY-ONE

Jackson

"He has us running in circles, chasing our tails," Brielle says when we're all back in Millie and Lucien's house, settled in the library. "And all the other metaphors I can think of. It's ridiculous."

"I would have sworn on my life that he was in that house," I say and hang my head in my hands. "I *know* that kitchen. I grew up in it. There was no mistaking it."

"Your premonitions have always been *could-bes*," Daphne points out. "A snapshot of what could be, not necessarily what *is*. And maybe it was something from years from now. We just don't know."

I sigh and nod, taking her hand in mine to kiss her fingers. "Yeah. I guess I got excited at the thought of stopping him."

"We're going to stop him," Millie reminds us. "Jack,

I mentioned blood magic earlier. To find him. To find the girls."

"I don't want to ask them," I admit, but Miss Sophia's head turns to me. She and Ruth sit by the fire, each making tea satchels. "They've been through a lot already because of me. I'd like to leave them out of this."

"And in doing so, you'll cut off a very powerful tool at your disposal," Miss Sophia says. "Jackson, Oliver and Annabelle are a part of your journey in this. They're tied to you, and I think it's lovely that you want to keep them safe, but you have to remember that they're the only parents you have. And they love you. If they can help, there's nothing they won't do."

"That's just it," I say and stand to pace. "There's *nothing* they won't do. They'd give their lives for mine, and I won't have that."

"Of course, not," Miss Sophia replies. "No one's asking that of them. But I know they'll help in any way they can."

"Where are they?" Millie asks. "I've hardly even known they're here."

"They've been spending a lot of time researching on their own," Ruth says. "Reading, meditating. Oliver is healing. They want to be as strong as possible for the battle to come. And they love you so much, Jackson. Give them the opportunity to help."

I take a deep breath. "I'll ask. We need to find the

women, so I'll ask. But we keep them safe. They don't leave this house. That's my line in the sand."

"Sweet boy," Miss Sophia says, cupping my face in her hands. "We won't let anyone hurt Oliver and Annabelle."

I nod and look over at Ruth. "Do you know where they are?"

"Last I saw them, they were enjoying the garden," she says with a smile.

"I'll be back."

I walk through the house and out the back door. Sure enough, they're sitting in the shade, each with a book in front of them, sipping some sweet tea.

"Well, hello there, darlin'," Miss Annabelle says with a smile. "How did it go?"

"We didn't find him." I sit across from them and lean on the table. "He's playing with us, and we're running out of time to save those women."

"How can we help?" Oliver asks without hesitation. He looks so much better than he did the day we brought him here. He's healthy and whole now, no longer tormented.

And I plan to keep it that way.

"Miss Annabelle, I know you have the gift of blood magic. I know opening yourself up can be dangerous, and I don't like to ask, but I'm going to. I think he's in the bayou. It's where he's the most comfortable. But the bayou is big, and I need help narrowing down his location."

"Of course," she says. "I need a map and a sterilized and charmed dagger. I'm sure we can get those things."

"Are you sure?" I reach over and take her hand. "We will do everything in our power to keep you safe. There are some pretty powerful witches in there."

"I've been a witch for a long time, my boy," she says with a soft smile. "I know what I'm about. I have you and Ollie here with me, my two loves. And my friends. I'll be safe. Now, let's go find those poor babies and get them home, shall we?"

SEVERAL HOURS LATER, we're set up around the dining room table. Candles are set around the room, and a large map of the bayou, a dagger that's been spelled with protections, and some other things I don't quite understand, sit on the surface.

Lucien swirls his finger in the air, and all of the candles light, casting the room in shadows.

"So cool," Daphne says with a grin. Lucien winks at her.

"I could learn to do that." I narrow my eyes at Lucien. "You have your own girl."

"That I do," he says with a laugh and kisses Millie's cheek.

Miss Sophia and Ruth flank Miss Annabelle, who lifts the dagger and begins to chant.

"North and south; east to west, blood to blood at my

behest. Show the way, flying free, location found, so mote it be."

Miss Annabelle holds up her hand and slices her palm, letting the blood fall on the map.

"Illuminate what we want to see. Lead us to those we must set free."

The blood swirls around the map and separates into droplets, scattering over the page. I look up at Lucien, whose face is creased in confusion.

Finally, Miss Annabelle wiggles her fingers and whispers something in Latin. The blood lifts into the air and then settles into a small vial that she seals and sets aside.

Oliver takes her hand in his, closes his eyes, and the wound heals.

"It didn't work," Daphne says and looks at Miss Annabelle with grief. "Why didn't it work?"

"Because this isn't my quest," Miss Annabelle replies. "My blood can't unlock what we need to see."

Immediately, Daphne thrusts her hand toward the other woman. "Take mine then. This *is* my quest."

I want to step in and say no. The thought of anyone deliberately cutting Daphne makes me crazy and stokes my need to defend her.

But I stay quiet.

Miss Annabelle begins the spell again, cuts Daphne's hand this time, and the blood drops onto the map. As Daphne pulls her hand away, Oliver takes it and, with a whisper, heals the wound.

"Illuminate what we want to see. Lead us to those we must set free," Miss Annabelle says again, and the blood begins to glow and move, this time in one circuit around the large map on the table.

When it settles onto one spot, everyone looks up at me.

"I *knew* it."

"There was nothing in that house," Cash says, shaking his head. "It's empty. Been abandoned for years."

"It's a spell," Lucien says. "He blinded us to what's really going on in there."

"We were *there*," Daphne whispers. "Oh, my goddess, we were there. The girls. We have to go back. How do we break the spell?"

"We have to hurry," Cash says. "And I'm calling Asher. He'll believe me. Hell, he was part of this before."

He leaves the room to make the call, and Miss Sophia and Miss Annabelle discuss different spells that might break the one Horace placed on my childhood home.

"Did he buy it?" I wonder aloud, catching Lucien's attention. "Did Horace buy the house all those years ago in preparation for this?"

"I doubt it." Lucien shakes his head. "He couldn't have known that things would end up like this. But it worked out well for him that no one has been in that house in a long time. I bet he got his rocks off when he discovered it."

"Let's move," Cash says as he returns to the room. "Asher's meeting us."

I PULL INTO THE DRIVEWAY, again ahead of Cash. I already see the difference.

"It doesn't look the same at all," Millie says in surprise. "There's a car in the driveway, and you can tell that someone's been in and out."

"The spell is already broken," Lucien says as we hurry to the front door. "And I'd wager that he's gone."

Cash turns to us and brushes his hand over his mouth. "I told Asher I'd wait, but damn it, those girls could be in there."

"Oh, they're in there," Brielle says. "And they're also standing behind me. But one is weird."

"How so?"

"She keeps coming and going. Flashing in and out. I don't know how else to describe it."

After just one more moment of hesitation, Cash looks us all dead in the eye.

"Don't touch anything. Nothing."

He opens the door, and we all file in behind him, frantically searching the space.

It's a fucking mess.

"The smell," Daphne says, covering her nose with her hand. "Oh, hell."

"That's a lot of death," I agree. We scout out the first floor and then make our way upstairs where Cash stands in a wide, double doorway. Both doors are open, and the scene beyond looks like something out of a horror movie.

"Don't go in," he says quietly. "We're too late."

I look over his shoulder and curse ripely.

"Jesus fucking Christ." I push my hands through my hair in agitation. "They're still bleeding, Cash."

"I see."

"We could have saved them. My God, we could have fucking saved them."

"No." Millie puts her hand on my shoulder gently. "He made sure that we couldn't."

"We have to be sure," Brielle says to Cash. "We have to check them. What if someone isn't dead?"

With a grim face, Cash nods, and we carefully make our way around the room. It's difficult to avoid stepping in blood, but Cash reminds us all again not to contaminate the scene.

My stomach jolts as I cross to a woman with red hair. She looks so similar to Daphne, it makes me nauseous.

When I reach down to touch her neck, just past the gash over it, she suddenly opens her eyes and gasps for breath, sitting up to my absolute shock and horror.

"Fucking hell," I exclaim and jump back right into a puddle of blood.

"Holy shit," Cash cries out as all three girls gasp. Lucien's eyes narrow.

The woman's blue eyes bulge. Her fiery red hair is full of blood, and she's coughing, clutching her chest as she gasps for breath.

"This is *insane,*" Daphne whispers and reaches for my hand.

When the woman stands, as naked as the day she was born, she narrows those eyes and walks through the bodies lying around her, toward us.

And that wound on her neck is closing. Healing as if it was never there.

"Who are you?" Brielle asks, stepping forward.

"Lucinda," the woman replies. "Lucy."

She pushes her hand into her hair, still looking around at the mess around her.

"I *knew* I recognized you," Millie says. "From the missing persons poster. You're Lucy Finch. From Salem."

"I am," Lucy says. "And I'm naked."

"And surprisingly calm," Daphne points out.

We hear footsteps below, and Cash turns to us.

"The cavalry is here. I'm going to be here for a while. Lucy, I need you to stay so I can ask some questions."

"I know," she says. "Can I cover up?"

"I have a blanket in the car," I offer and run down

past the cops to my vehicle, retrieving the throw and hurrying back up with it.

Then the five of us are ushered out while the police take over.

"At least Cash is in there," Millie says. "So we know what's happening."

"Who is Lucy Finch?" Daphne asks her sister. "And why did she miraculously come back from the dead, scaring the shit out of us before our very eyes?"

"She's a witch—a powerful one from what I've heard. I've never met her. She's related to some of the witches in Baton Rouge. They must have invited her to come join us for the eclipse. I have no idea why she's *here*-here, or how she didn't die."

"Maybe she *did* somehow die and then came back to life," Brielle adds. "Because she's the one who was blinking in and out."

"We'll get to the bottom of it," Lucien says. "Also, I found Andy."

"Where?" I demand as I turn to him.

"He's in the bathroom upstairs. Dead. Missing his eyes. I told Cash on our way out."

"Why didn't you say something before?" Brielle demands.

"Because you three don't need to see that," Lucien says softly. "There's no need. You already have enough terror in your minds."

"He's right," Millie says. "I don't want to see it."

"Me, either."

Cash comes outside, escorting Lucy, who's wrapped in the blanket. She doesn't look freaked out. She looks...pissed.

"I don't need a hospital," she insists.

"Your throat was slashed," Cash says.

"It's not now. Look." She points to her neck. "Not even a scar. I want to talk to you all. I can help you."

"You need a shower," Millie says. "And some fresh clothes."

"Damn right, I do," Lucy agrees.

Cash doesn't look convinced.

"I promise you. I don't need a hospital. I also promise that I have no intention of hurting any of you. I came here to help. I wanted a fun trip to New Orleans and to help you all at the same time. We can see how that worked out for me."

"Did he know?" I demand. "Did he know what you are?"

"No. I never let on. I promise I can tell you everything. But I'm sure you can understand why I'm anxious to get the hell out of here."

"Let's take her back," Millie says. "Get her cleaned up—physically and spiritually."

"If you're fucking with them," Cash says quietly, "this will end very badly for you."

Lucy's face softens. "You love them. Of course, you do. You're the six. I wish you no harm."

Cash takes a deep breath and then nods. "Okay. I have to stay here for a bit longer, but I'll meet you at the house. I'll catch a ride with one of the guys."

Lucy rides with Daphne and me. She's quiet, curled up in the back seat the whole way.

When we pull up to Millie's house, she smiles.

"How lovely."

Before we leave the car, Daphne turns to Lucy.

"How do I know that you're not *him*? That you're not Horace, worming his way into this house to hurt us?"

"Horace can't get inside of that house," Lucy says calmly. "I understand your concern. I'd be wary, as well. When you found me, I was pretty much dead."

"Are you immortal?" I ask her.

"No." She smiles again. "I'm just a woman with magic. I promise you, I'm not your enemy. I will not hurt you."

I look at Daphne, and she nods. We escort Lucy into the house where Miss Sophia, Ruth, Oliver, and Miss Annabelle are all waiting.

When they see Lucy, there's a frenzy.

"Oh, you poor child," Ruth says as she reaches for Lucy. When she touches Lucy's shoulder, Lucy jerks.

"What is it?" Millie asks her.

"Oh, ma'am," Lucy says as tears fill her eyes. "I'm so sorry for what was done to you. I'm so, so sorry."

"This is Lucy Finch," Lucien explains. "She was being held by Horace. Managed to live through it and came all the way from Salem to help us."

"Well, you come on in," Miss Annabelle says. "We'll get you cleaned up and comfortable before anyone starts asking questions."

"I'll fix some soup," Millie announces and heads for the kitchen.

"I have some clothes that should fit you," Daphne says, eyeing the other woman. "He took you because you look like me."

Lucy nods. "I know."

"I'm sorry."

"It's not your fault," Lucy assures Daphne. "It's not your fault at all. I could use that shower."

"I'll take you up," Daphne says and takes Lucy's hand before stopping cold, her wide eyes meeting Lucy's. "Oh, Lucy."

"Let's go up," Lucy suggests. "And then we'll talk about it."

CHAPTER TWENTY-TWO

Daphne

I can hear her in the shower. She's been in there for more than thirty minutes. Frankly, I don't blame her.

She may scrub off the blood, but she'll never forget what it felt like on her skin.

I'd want to wash until I was raw.

I've never been so scared as I was when Lucy's eyes opened, and she sat up. What kind of crazy zombie movie am I living in anyway?

The water shuts off, and another fifteen minutes tick by before Lucy pokes her head out of the steamy bathroom.

She's dressed in a pair of my leggings and a T-shirt. Her clean hair is wet and twisted up and out of her face.

"You look like a college co-ed," I say with a smile. "And you'd never know a serial killer spirit held you captive for a couple of days."

Her smile is thin and she looks exhausted. "I know he did. It all started to catch up to me in the shower, and I had a good crying jag."

"Honey, you can cry all you want," I inform her. "Cry it all out."

"It won't help anything." She shrugs. "Thanks for loaning me the clothes."

"It's honestly the very least I can do. I have so many questions, Lucy." I want to reach out and hug her. The touch a little while ago had shown me so much—more than I usually see when I touch people.

Again, it's not people who tell me stories. It's *things.*

"I know you do," she says. "Everyone does. Let's go downstairs, and I'll answer all of the questions."

"I'm pretty sure Millie probably made you all kinds of soup and tea with special cleansing and protection spells in them."

"That will be lovely." We set out down the hall to the stairs. "You're a powerful sensitive, Daphne. Psychometric?"

I raise a brow. "Yes. But lately, I've been picking up on people's emotions, as well. Seeing more. It's unusual for me."

"I suspect it's because so much is happening right now and it's igniting your gifts. Amplifying them. You may have always been a little psychic in that way and didn't really notice until now."

"Maybe you're right."

We get to the bottom of the steps, and I hear everyone in the library.

"We've been gathering in here for meetings," I tell Lucy as I lead her to the others. "It's my favorite room in the house."

She smiles when we reach the threshold. "What's not to love about a room so full of books? Is Millie Belle from *Beauty and the Beast*?"

"You're my kind of people," Millie says with a wink. "And, yes, I often go on rides on the sliding ladder. Come on in. I have hot soup and tea for you. And anything else you might need."

"A cozy spot to sit would be blissful," Lucy says and sighs in relief when she plops down in a plush chair and then pulls a throw blanket over her lap.

Sanguine jumps into Lucy's lap, turns three circles, and curls up to sleep.

"Wow," Millie says in surprise. "Sanguine is my familiar and doesn't usually take to strangers so quickly."

"What a beautiful name for such a pretty girl," Lucy coos and scratches the cat's ears. "She knows that I miss my familiar back home. Nera got me through the last few days without losing my mind."

"Your familiar was with you?" I ask.

"Oh, yes. Spiritually, anyway. He's been sick with worry, but he's calm now. He's an Irish Wolfhound. My big, gentle giant. And a fierce knight, just like his namesake."

Lucy smiles at Millie, who sets a tray of soup and tea before her.

"All of this has protection and cleansing potions added. It shouldn't make it taste bad. I think you need it."

"I do. Thank you."

Lucy reaches for the tea, sits back, and meets Miss Sophia's gaze.

The library is dark, with candles lit around the spacious room. Everyone is here, including Lucien's parents and Cash, who must have arrived while I was upstairs with Lucy.

It's a packed house.

And we're all trying to give Lucy space to settle in before we pounce on her and pepper her with questions.

"You and I have met before," Lucy says to Miss Sophia. "I was a young girl, and you and your sister came to Boston to help with a missing persons case. You came to Salem for a day."

"Yes, I remember," Miss Sophia replies. "I told your mother when I saw you that you were an old soul. That you see and know more than anyone realizes."

"I'd say that's still true," Lucy says. "We lost Mama last year. But she always had kind things to say about you. Now, I'm sure you all have questions, and there are some things that I *have* to tell you."

"Not too much," Miss Sophia advises, and we all

frown at her. "Some of it they have to figure out for themselves."

"I know," Lucy says with a nod. "But there's much that I *can* say, and knowledge is power. I'll just start at the beginning, if that's okay. Otherwise, I'll get all turned around. My mind is clearing, but it's still kind of jumbled, too."

"Just take your time," Mama says kindly. "You drink that tea and take your time."

Lucy nods and sips her tea.

"I arrived in New Orleans a day earlier than when we were supposed to meet to go over the plan with you all. I wanted to soak in the city a bit before the eclipse. I've been here several times, and it's one of my favorite places. Anyway, I went out for dinner the night I arrived."

"Alone?" Cash asks.

"Yes. I don't mind being by myself. Especially in this city. I had a delicious meal and a couple of glasses of wine. I wasn't drunk. I left the restaurant and strolled down the street, peeking into gallery windows and being lazy about walking back to my hotel. I wasn't in a rush. Then, suddenly, a man brushed past me and stuck me with a syringe. Drugged me."

She sips her tea again.

"He pulled me into a waiting car. I noticed he was alone, but then I passed out. And let me just say, I'm still confused because I have some powerful spells for protection, yet he was able to take me."

"He's a powerful witch in his own right," Millie says.

"Yes. He is." Lucy clears her throat. "When I woke up, I was in that house. With the other girls. One was dead when I woke. I tried so hard to cast some spells to protect the others, but it didn't work. It was like something blocked my magic in there."

"It very well could have been," Miss Annabelle adds. "I know you don't know any of us, and we'll introduce ourselves later, just know that all of us are part of the coven, and you're safe here. I only wanted to add that he likely did cast a spell on that house to ward off any kind of witch."

"I felt powerless," Lucy admits softly and stares down into her tea. "And I knew that I couldn't let on that I was a witch because, well...you know why. He would have made it hell for me. Even more than it already was. Anyway, we heard you earlier today. We heard you walking through the house. The other girls screamed for you, pled for you to save us."

"But he'd cast a spell, preventing us from seeing or hearing anything," Lucien says, frustration in his voice. "We were right *there*. I'm so sorry."

"He was furious," Lucy continues with a shiver. "He ranted and raved, stomped around. And then he killed everyone.

"Before that, when he killed a girl, he was always calm about it. Methodical. He clearly enjoyed it. But today, he killed in a rage. I was the last."

She blinks, then frowns.

"How did you come back to life?" Brielle asks. "How did you heal that wound on your throat?"

Lucy smiles softly and turns, pointing to the tattoo on the back of her neck before turning back to us.

"I assume each of you has an affinity. A gift. Daphne's is psychometry." She smiles at me. "I cast a spell on this tattoo. It prevents me from dying at the hands of anything supernatural."

The room is silent. Finally, Miss Sophia stands and crosses to Lucy, examining the tattoo on the younger woman's neck.

"I've heard of this magic before," Miss Sophia says. "Whispers, anyway. But we believe that we shouldn't interfere in life and death, so it's not something I've ever pursued."

"It's a spell that can only be cast once for each person," Lucy says. "So, I cast it on this tattoo. I'll never lose it. And I agree, we can't interfere with life and death. But there are some crazy things afoot in Salem, and ninety-nine percent of them aren't human. I needed the added protection."

"I wonder," Millie says, tapping her lips with her finger. "Could this spell be cast on stones? To protect the witches who are coming here to help us? He'll try to kill them tomorrow."

"I'm sure I can do that," Lucy says with a nod.

Suddenly, Millie's eyes widen, and she looks at Lucien. I can see they're having a telepathic conversation.

"We've never tried that before," Lucien says thoughtfully. "Never in any other lifetime. It could work."

"What could work?" Brielle demands.

"I need to do some quick reading," Lucien says as he stands and hurries from the room.

"You're all so interesting," Lucy says and spoons up some soup. "I have so many questions, but there's no time. We have twenty-four hours until the eclipse."

Millie turns to Miss Sophia, who now has a broad smile on her beautiful face.

"You've figured it out," she says as tears fill her eyes. "I'm so proud of you."

"WE NEED THIS TIME TOGETHER," Millie says. The three of us are up in the attic of Millie's house, sitting in the same spot we had when Millie showed us the hiding hole where she found the items hidden from her past life.

The rest of the house is quiet. Lucien is reading, and Jackson and Cash are talking quietly in the library.

Miss Sophia and the others went to bed. Even Lucien's parents decided to spend the night. We're all safe and under one roof.

Our sanctuary.

"This house is huge," I inform my sister. "I mean, I

knew it was big, but we have thirteen people sleeping here tonight, and there is room for all of them."

"The inn is officially full," Millie says with a laugh. "We're at capacity. But I'm grateful that we have the space. This would have been much more difficult without it."

We hear a door slam downstairs. Twice.

Then some scraping along the floor in the attic.

"She's been more active," Brielle says as she seems to watch something move through the attic. "Your ghost. She's not just unhappy at having so many people here. She's also looking out for you and Lucien. I don't think she was related to you before. She just feels responsible for you. She's protective."

A door slams again, and we suddenly hear a baby crying.

"I hear the baby," I say in surprise.

"I can, too," Millie whispers. "Yes, things are ramping up, that's for sure. The energy surrounding the house is just massive. I feel as if my skin is vibrating with it. But it doesn't feel like bad energy. It's protective."

"My abilities are ramping up, too," I confide. "I can feel emotions now. I can't read thoughts like Millie can when she lowers her shields, but things are definitely growing and changing. Like my psyche is getting ready for tomorrow."

"It's happening with me, too," Brielle says. "I should also add that the girls are gone now. As soon as we got to the house earlier and found them all, they stopped following me."

"Thank goodness." I run my hand down Brielle's long, dark hair. "I hate that they followed you. It's just damn creepy."

"All of this is creepy," Brielle says with a sigh. "I want to talk about tomorrow night."

"No." I shake my head. "I don't want to overthink it. To overanalyze. We have a plan, a very good one thanks to Lucien, and I know it's going to work. I don't want to keep talking about it over and over again."

"I don't want to pick apart the plan," Brielle says with a scowl. "That's not what I meant. I just wanted to say that I think we should open the doorway between our minds the way Millie and Lucien do with each other. We need to be linked at all times during the eclipse. This asshole likes to separate us. Confuse us. We can't let him do that."

"Okay, I agree with that," I reply with a nod. "I want to be able to reach out to each of you with my mind."

"We can do that," Millie says. "It's a simple spell. Lucien will help."

We're quiet for a long moment, soaking in our love for each other and the noises in the house.

"This reminds me of when we were kids." I reach out for Brielle's hand. "When we'd hide under the stairs."

"I hate that house," Millie whispers. "I've never hated anything the way I do that house."

"And none of us ever has to go back there. We aren't vulnerable little girls anymore," Brielle reminds us. "We're powerful witches. And this son of a bitch underestimated our power."

"Damn right," Millie says and covers our hands with hers. "We will come out the other side of this."

"What will we do then? I don't remember a time he *didn't* torment us."

Brielle blinks at my question. "You're right. Well, I guess we'll figure it out. But the most important thing is, he'll be gone, and we can do whatever the hell we want."

JUST A COUPLE OF HOURS LATER, I slip quietly into the bedroom in case Jackson is already asleep. Millie coached Brielle and me through some meditations, and we spent time together, getting stronger.

We've always been strong together.

We're even more so with our men.

After I close the door as silently as possible, I turn around to find Jack sitting in a chair by the window, a book in his lap, and a candle burning at his elbow.

"Hey." I grin and hurry over to him, sitting in his lap. "I thought you might be asleep."

"I was waiting for you," he says and nuzzles my neck. "What were you girls doing for so long?"

"Just sister stuff."

He waggles his eyebrows, and I scoff, smacking him in the shoulder. "You're such a pervert."

"I didn't say anything."

I laugh and glance down at his book. "What are you studying?"

"I'm resubmerging myself in the magic—the craft. I remember a lot of this, but there's plenty that I don't. Lucien has been giving me pointers when we're not being interrupted by a psychotic being."

"Which is all the time," I add, kissing his forehead. "The more armed you are, the better, Jack."

"I figured that, as well." He grins. "Want to see something cool?"

"Always."

"Okay, I have to move you." He takes me by the hips and pushes me to my feet, then leans over and blows out the candle, making the bedroom go dark.

In the moonlight, I see Jack swirl his finger. Then, suddenly, the candle lights once more.

"Okay, that's the *coolest* thing." I lean into him, wrapping my arms around his middle. "And, I have to admit, quite sexy."

"I'm done watching your eyes light up every time Lucien does it." I glance up, and his eyes narrow on me.

"You were never a jealous man before."

His lips twitch into a grin. "Yes, I was. I just never needed to be because you never looked at anyone like that except *me*."

"I don't look at Lucien in any way. I like the parlor

tricks he can do. It doesn't mean I want to jump his bones or anything. Millie would not approve."

"Neither would Jackson." He picks me up, sits in the chair once more, and settles me back in his lap.

"What other things have you learned?" I brush my fingers through his dark hair. I always did love how it felt against my skin.

"A little of this." He kisses my neck. "A little of that. Mostly, I'm learning to drop the shields I've had in place for so many years and control myself when they're down. A lot of this is about control. Having a strong mind."

"Speaking of a strong mind." I tell him about the telepathic link I want to establish with the others, and he listens intently.

"So, we'll be able to read each other's thoughts?"

"Yes. And speak to each other without having to say anything at all verbally. Only for a few hours, of course."

"I'm in."

"That simple?"

"That simple." He kisses my jawline. It's as though he can't keep his lips off me, and I'm not complaining.

Sex is powerful magic all on its own.

But before I have the chance to start getting him naked, he pulls back again and looks at me with serious eyes.

"What is it?" I ask.

"You said before that you're scared. Of all of this. Are you still?"

I rub my lips together, still tasting him there as I think it over. "It's not that I'm scared of what's going to happen tomorrow night. I'm a little nervous, but mostly I'm ready to get this show on the road and kick Horace's ass. So, no, that's not what I'm afraid of. Mostly, I'm scared that you'll be gone—"

"I've told you a million times that I'm not going to walk away. How many times do you need me to reassure you—?"

"Let me finish." I lay my finger over his lips, shushing him. "I know you won't walk away. What I'm saying is, it would kill me if, during everything that happens tomorrow night, he hurt you. Killed you somehow. I don't think I'd survive it, Jack."

"Hey." He cups my face and kisses me so tenderly that it brings tears to my eyes. "He won't kill me. Any of us."

I nod, needing to believe him. I can't go into it with the fear of one of us dying.

I need to have the utmost confidence that nothing will go wrong.

"I just got you back." His words are a whisper. "And I don't plan to ever let you go again, Daph. We're soulmates. We're linked. You're meant for me. You are, in every way that counts, my wife."

I raise my eyebrows in surprise.

"Oh, come on. We don't need a ritual to know what we are to each other. Now, I know that we'll do that.

When all of this is said and done, I'll be asking you a very important question."

I feel the smile spread across my face.

"But we're as linked, and our love is as strong as Cash and Brielle's or Millie and Lucien's. You know that."

"Yeah." I shift so I can straddle him and loop my arms around his neck. "Yeah, I know it. You're mine, and I'm yours. For all time. Do you know another tool for making us extra strong for tomorrow night?"

"What's that?"

"Sex." I bite his lower lip as he smiles. "Sex magic is quite powerful, you know."

"The way we do it, it most certainly is." He lifts me and crosses to the bed, lowering me onto it. "We'll make sure to get some extra magic tonight, sweets."

CHAPTER TWENTY-THREE

Jackson

It's been a morning of salt baths, herb burning, and more meditations than I've ever done in my life. There can be no mistakes today, and the six of us—along with those we love who came to help—need all the witchy assistance we can get.

The field behind Miss Sophia's house is alive with activity. Two big, white tents have been set up with tables and chairs, and each is full of supplies for the dozens—maybe a hundred?—witches who've come from all over to help us.

Lucy stands next to a table with Mallory Boudreaux. They managed to accumulate hundreds of pieces of black tourmaline, and Lucy is busy casting her immortality spell on all of them.

When she's finished, she turns and yells so everyone can hear her.

"I want you all to come and choose a piece of this

schorl. You can have any piece that speaks to you. It will protect you tonight. Don't lose it."

I brush my fingers over the auralite stone that Daphne gave me just a couple of weeks ago. Has it only been that long? It feels like months.

Where are you?

I smile at the sound of Daphne's voice in my head. This morning, after meditation and coffee, Lucien led us in the spell that opened our minds to each other. It's better than any cell phone service.

In the farthest tent. Headed back toward the house now.

I walk past several people I used to know when I was a child and stop to say hello, shaking hands and offering hugs.

I'm grateful. That's what it boils down to. All of these people took time out of their lives, some even traveled thousands of miles to be here with the six of us. To help us face the toughest battle of our lives.

How do you repay something like that?

"I know you have plenty of pieces of protection on you," Miss Claudette, an elderly woman who has to be in her nineties says as I pass. "But I put some extra blessings on this worry stone. Just tuck it into your pocket."

"Thank you, Miss Claudette." I lean down and kiss her wrinkled cheek, slipping the smooth stone into my pocket as I turn to go and find my love.

Suddenly, the edges of my sight turn gray, and I know I'm being sucked into a vision—a premonition.

Wind. So much wind, I can hardly catch my breath. He's trying to fight us, to keep us from being able to defend ourselves against him. I hear screams, but they're not human.

So many spirits rush around us—his army, doing their best to frighten and disarm.

But we're not in Miss Sophia's field. We're standing before Daphne's childhood home. Lights flash like lightning inside the house. Shutters fling about, and shadow spirits float in and out, all around the old house.

"The new moon phase is here," I hear Lucien shout. "Everyone, take your marks!"

Suddenly, we're plunged into darkness when the shadow of the Earth completely covers the moon, turning it an ominous red.

Lucien lights the torches with the wave of his arms, Millie raises her hands high and directs the wind.

We hear a horrible scream, and then, suddenly, we're under attack by wolves, ravens, and bats. I watch in horror as an enormous gray wolf charges Daphne and bites her throat, tackling her to the ground.

"Jackson?"

I blink and frown at Lucien.

"We need to talk with the others," I say immediately. God, my heart is hammering, and I've broken out in a sweat. "We have this all wrong, Lucien."

"We have two hours," he says, his voice full of frustration. "What do you mean we have it *wrong*?"

"Wait. We're linked, but you couldn't see the premonition?"

He just shakes his head in frustration.

I need all of you. I reach out with my mind, calling to the others. *Meet me at the house.*

Lucien and I jog across the field and meet up with Cash and the women.

"It's damn weird having y'all in my head," Cash says and props his hands on his hips.

"What's wrong?" Daphne asks.

"You look horrible," Brielle adds, scowling at me.

"I had a vision." I take a deep breath, trying to calm my heart rate. "We can't do this here. Not here. Not at Miss Sophia's. It has to be at the old house. At your childhood house."

Daphne goes pale and shakes her head. "No."

"It makes sense," Lucien says. "It started there. It should end there."

"I hate that you're right," Millie says and shares a look with her sisters. She reaches for Daphne's hand. "We can do this. It's going to be okay. We have to alert the others. We have to get over there right away and set up. I think the sound system is ready to go."

"Someone brought a sound system?" I ask Cash as Millie rushes away.

"It's easier to talk to a hundred witches with a microphone," he says with a nod.

"I need your attention," Millie says. She holds a black mic and waves her free arm to get everyone's attention. "We have to move our location."

She explains what needs to happen, and I expect

everyone to groan and be irritated, but that's not the case at all.

I see nods of agreement. Immediately, everyone works together to gather the tools we'll need, loading them into cars so we can hurry to the other house.

Thankfully, it's less than ten minutes away.

"Before we go," Millie says to everyone, "you need to know that this house is the epicenter of something truly evil. It's dangerous. Keep your shields up. Be careful. Blessed be."

We hurry to our vehicles. When Daphne and I are in the car and on the road, I glance over to see that she's still as pale as a ghost, and her hands are fisted in her lap, her knuckles white.

"Hey, talk to me, sweets."

"You don't understand," she whispers. "That house is the biggest source of terror in my life. It's horrible, Jack. Not to mention, my father's spirit is there. I don't know if I can do this."

"Stop it." I take her hand and pull it to my lips. "You've been told, several times now, that the key to stopping your father is in you. That you need to stand up for yourself. Confront the bully."

"Easy to say when it isn't *you* he's bullying."

"That's true enough. You won't be alone, though, Daph. You have about a hundred witches with you. You're a badass woman. You're not the shy, unsure young lady I met at that Samhain party all those years ago. You're strong, and you're fucking amazing. I have every confidence that you're going to kick some serious ass today."

"Thanks." She takes a deep breath and then lets it out slowly. "I needed that pep talk."

I love you, she says silently.

I love you, too.

We step out of the car and immediately hit a paranormal barrier. It's like walking into a twenty-five-foot wall of water.

Shields, Millie says in our heads. *Keep them up.*

The others follow us and park anywhere there's empty space, then immediately begin casting spells to push back the energy.

The six of us flank Ruth, who stands before the house, her head tilted as she examines it with wide, blue eyes.

The four women join hands.

We watch as shadows stand on the roof, on the porch. As lights flicker inside without the help of electricity.

They turned that off long ago.

I hear moaning and maniacal laughter. Banging and scraping.

All coming from the house.

"How did I live there for so long?" Ruth wonders aloud.

"Mama, you stay strong," Brielle says. "Nothing in there can get to you while we're here with you."

"I'm not worried about that, child," Ruth says

calmly. "I'm just thinking. I've known since I came to stay with Sophia that I would play a part in this. Why else would he have handicapped me for so many years? Made certain I couldn't protect you?"

I frown down at Ruth. "You think it was Horace's doing? That your possession all those years was because of him?"

"I know it was," she says flatly. "I know it now, anyway. I'm stronger now. I have tools, especially after many long hours going through everything with Sophia. And I have my girls and their brave men. I know what I have to do. But in order to do it, I have to get inside this house."

"No."

"Absolutely not."

"You're out of your mind."

We're all speaking at once, absolutely opposed to Ruth going inside.

"Girls." Ruth holds up her hand. "I need something from in there. Something that was my grandmother's. I know precisely where it is."

"If it's upstairs, you can't get to it," Millie says. "That staircase isn't sound."

"It's under the stairs by the back door," Ruth replies. "I know you girls hid under there sometimes. I don't know how I know, I just do. I hid a box of things under there for safekeeping. I need that box."

"It's right inside the back door," Brielle murmurs.

"Maybe we can get around the house, sneak in the back way, and grab it really quickly."

"There's no sneaking." I gesture to the hundreds of shadows currently staring at us. "They're watching every move we make. And I'll wager a guess that Horace is in there watching, too."

"I need that box," Ruth says again. "I'll go in and get it myself."

"No." Lucien lays his hand on Ruth's shoulder. "We can't let you go in there, Ruth."

He turns to the rest of us with a sigh.

"We'll get it," he continues. "The six of us together. From here on out, we stand as one. We're stronger together."

"We're going to walk right through the back door," Cash agrees. "No apologies. No fear. What's in there belongs to Ruth, and she'll have it."

"Now isn't exactly the moment I'd choose to get all in your face about this," Daphne says with a sigh, "but fine. We go. In and out. We don't have much time before the eclipse begins."

"Come with me," Miss Sophia says to Ruth, taking her hand and pulling her back with the others.

Hand-in-hand, the six of us take off around the house.

Ignore them, Lucien says in our heads. *The spirits will try to scare us off. Ignore them.*

It's a little hard to do when they're pushing and grabbing, doing everything they can to terrorize us.

I see Daddy, Daphne says. Even telepathically, her voice shakes. *In the garden.*

I just saw him looking out of a window, Millie adds.

More games, Lucien says.

We push through the back door, taking it clear off the rusted hinges, and Brielle opens the small door that leads to the space under the stairs.

"I see it," she cries. Seconds later, she and Cash hurry out, each carrying a handle on the side of an old trunk.

"Let me," I say and take Brielle's end. "It's damn heavy."

"Let's go!" Daphne yells, and we hurry back around the house. Ruth's face lights up when she sees that we found her trunk.

"Oh, thank you. Thank you so much." She falls to her knees and opens the lid, shuffling through the treasures inside. As she and Sophia put their heads together, the six of us huddle up.

It's game time.

The moon is waning, Lucien says. *It's time to put this plan into motion.*

He waves his arm and lights all the torches that have been set up around the front of the house. I'm surprised as I look around at how much has been done in just a few minutes.

Witches work damn fast when they have to.

The crowd of witches standing behind us is an army I'm proud to fight with and for. Some are literally dressed for battle with protective gear and helmets. Others are dressed casually, holding wands or crystals.

More still look like the witches you'd see in the movies, wearing cloaks, standing before cauldrons with large crystal balls in the palms of their hands.

No matter the skill they're using, no matter what they look like, each one uses their affinity to help us to the best of their ability.

Lucy steps forward wearing a red shroud, a grimoire in her hands.

"I'm going to lead the others in the spells you taught us this morning," she says to us, her eyes never leaving the house behind us. "We will need the help of the goddess and all the deities to fight this. I've never seen anything like it."

"And you never will again," Lucien says. "Thank you."

He turns back to us, *into* us, and raises his athame high, turning to each of the four cardinal directions and calling upon the watchtowers while whispering words of invocation before walking the perimeter behind us, starting in the north.

"Element of earth, we call on you. Lend us your strength and keep us grounded in our task." He walks to the east. "Element of air, we call upon you. Let us be flexible in our ways but powerful in our might." He rounds to the south. "Element of fire, we beseech thee. Lend us your power and passion to overcome our foes." Facing the west, he says, "Element of water, we ask your assistance. Show us your might and buoy us in our fight."

When he returns to his place in the circle, he reaches out to grab the hands of those on either side of him, and all of us follow suit with our neighbors, creating a spiral of energy around the circle. "We enter this space in perfect love and perfect trust. The circle is cast. No negative energies may enter this space, and any already within are subject to our will. Raising the infinite power of three times three, so it is, so mote it be."

The wind picks up around us as the moon continues to fade with the shadow of the Earth. Suddenly, lightning illuminates the top of the house, and there stands Horace.

Waiting

Watching.

"He looks like he did before," Brielle yells out above the sound of the wind. "When he was alive!"

"He's manifested himself back into being," Millie says.

It means he's strong. Stronger than ever.

But then, so are we.

"We are the six, the six are we..." We begin the spell for the waning moon, pulling in protection and strength from the deities and using it to create powerful banishing magic.

It pisses off everything in and around that house—even more than creating the circle did.

Horace's voice booms down from above.

"You will not defeat me! How dare you? HOW DARE YOU!"

More lightning, thunder, and wind. The shadows run and fly about in agitation, but because of the spells being cast behind us, they can't reach us.

They're like dogs, feral, nasty canines in a cage, snarling and spitting.

The new moon phase is seconds away, Brielle says in our heads.

The second stage of our plan is being set in motion. I plant my feet, grit my teeth, and get ready for the battle of my life.

As the moon plunges us into complete darkness, we begin the next spell.

"By the dark of the moon, in the shadow of Earth, we manifest our desires and give intention new birth. Lord and Lady, lend us your might; stop this evil and make everything right. Our power is yours, as well it should be. Let yours be ours, so mote it be."

The wind before was *nothing* compared to this. It swirls and circles around us, and I can feel the good fighting the bad energy, the spiritual warfare taking place all around us.

Ruth sits just in front of us, a black mirror clutched in her hands as she begins to scry. I've never seen anyone do it before, but I know exactly what this is.

Brielle moves forward to get her mother, to pull her back to safety, but Millie stops her.

She's our key, Millie says. *She's going to open the gateway to the other side for us. It's the only way!*

She could be killed, Daphne cries.

She won't be, Cash adds.

And so, Ruth continues, putting herself into a trance with the black mirror.

Suddenly, an onslaught of animals charges toward us and the others behind us. Wolves, ravens, bats, and snakes, all hell-bent on stopping everything we're doing.

Witches cry out in pain, dying in horrible slaughter. But then they gasp, the way Lucy did yesterday, and stand back up again.

Horace rages.

I watch in horror as a gray wolf charges Daphne.

Just like it did in my premonition.

But it doesn't take her down. To my utter shock and delight, she holds up a hand, and the wolf stops in its tracks, whimpering before it disappears.

She looks to her right and stops cold. A huge wolf didn't scare her in the least, but whatever she sees now has her face pale, and her hands clenched into fists at her sides.

I follow her gaze.

Her father.

Only you can stop him, I remind her telepathically. *You're not a little girl anymore, Daphne.*

She takes a deep breath, tightening her jaw, and I know that she's ready to kick that motherfucker's ass.

CHAPTER TWENTY-FOUR

Daphne

It's as if all of the chaos around me is suddenly just...gone.

All I can see is him.

The man who's tormented me for all of my life—first when he was alive, and then from beyond the grave. The one just yards from where I stand, in the rose garden beside the house.

He smiles and shows me those awful teeth, his eyes full of gleeful torment.

And then he starts walking right toward me.

"You can't hurt me anymore, you piece of shit," I yell. "You can't *scare* me!"

Suddenly, he reaches out and wraps his hands around my neck. He can *touch* me. He can hurt me.

He squeezes.

I hear the others around me, yelling and fighting off the animals and shadows.

And for just a brief moment, I can't breathe.

That awful mouth widens as he squeezes harder. For a moment, I'm so terrified, I just freeze.

You're not a little girl. It's Jackson's voice in my head. Oh, Goddess, what if I never see him again. What if this man kills me, after all? And all of this is for nothing.

We lose.

"No." I grip his wrists in my hands and use all my energy. The fire spell that Lucien sends into my head takes shape, and I burn the son of a bitch.

He recoils, and I fall to my feet.

"You can't hurt me anymore. You're *nothing*, Adam Landry. You have no place here—at this house, or anywhere else. The only place you belong is in the dirt."

I'm walking forward, pushing him back. So many years of anger fuel me, so much frustration and hurt and sadness.

"I don't know what we ever did to you to deserve this horror, but it's *over.* Do you understand me? It's done."

We're standing in the rose bushes. The one place on this Earth that once filled me with more terror than any other in my life.

But not anymore.

"You're dead. I'm alive. There's nothing you can do to change that."

I hold up my hands and feel a new wind swirl around me, pushing energy into me, through me as fuel. It could be coming from the army behind me or the other five. Maybe both.

Or perhaps it's *my* magic. Power that has always been inside of me. Something I didn't even know I had. I feel it building, pushing me.

I shove him, physically push my father back down to the earth and use a little spell that I learned years ago in my early days with the coven.

A simple one that's been with me all of these years.

"You've sent me strife and brought me pain. None of this shall be again. Off you go, you must flee. I turn this torment back on thee. As I will it, so mote it be."

Over and over, I repeat the spell as he writhes and cries and is absorbed back into the earth.

Back into his grave.

When I look up, I see the five now surround me as the other witches pour salt counterclockwise in a circle.

"Good girl," Jackson murmurs and kisses my forehead. "Now, for the grand finale."

"Not quite yet," Lucien says grimly as we retake our places. More salt is poured. Candles carved with ritual symbols are set out. Once in place, Lucien lights them all. "First, we have to summon more of an army. He won't go gently into this not-so-quiet night."

"The animals are gone," I say in surprise.

"You were a little busy with other things," Millie says with a wink. "The moon is waxing now. It's time to call on the deities and summon the spirits."

I don't know these spells by heart, but I open myself

and raise my hands with the others, watching as the sky opens above us. It's like something out of a movie.

Jackson's parents are suddenly there, along with our grandmother. People we must have known in previous lives.

Even men in uniform, Jack's fellow soldiers that he lost in battle, they are all with us.

But if we're able to summon, so is Horace.

And he has.

The ground trembles, the earth shifts and lifts, and suddenly swallows the house whole, right before our very eyes.

More shadows than I've ever seen before pour out of what must be the gates of hell, the place the house once stood, crawling like spiders and slithering like snakes.

Our families surround us now, all of them standing close by. Oliver and Miss Annabelle stand behind Jackson. Gwyneth and Aiden with Lucien. We have Miss Sophia and our coven family right here with us, too.

Mama's sweating, but she's still in her trance, her scrying mirror clutched firmly in her hands.

And when the moon is full and bright once more, she begins to shout.

"The door is open!" she cries. "It's time!"

The six of us join hands, and as chaos reigns around us, as the spirits we've summoned fight the demons, we step through the doorway that Mama unlocked and begin our final spell.

"Lords of the watchtowers of the east,

Lords of air,

We do summon, call and stir you up

To witness our rites and guard our circle!

Lords of the watchtowers of the south,

Lords of fire,

We do summon, call and stir you up

To witness our rites and guard our circle!

Lords of the watchtowers of the west,

Lords of water,

We do summon, call and stir you up

To witness our rites and guard our circle!

Lords of the watchtowers of the north,

Lords of earth,

We do summon, call and stir you up

To witness our rites and guard our circle!

Mother Earth, we call on you!

Father Sky, we call on you!"

Horace appears before us, pacing and shaking his head.

"It won't work," he says, his voice taunting. "You can't be rid of me, girls. No matter what you try or where you go, I'll always be here. Ready to punish you. Ready to remind you of who you are and everything you can be. Why are you making this so hard?"

While he throws his tantrum, the six of us check in with each other, through our minds.

Are we ready?

Yes.

Absolutely.

Without a doubt.

We will end him.

"It could have been beautiful," he continues and then turns a charming smile on the three of us. Zeroing in on me. "Daphne. You're so sweet. So loving. I know that you don't want to do this."

Play along, I tell the others.

"I think I have to." I make my voice shaky. "My sisters told me that I have to."

"They're wrong," he says and clucks his tongue. "You don't have to listen to them, Daphne. We can make them see what we do. That we're better together. That the four of us can be together and it'll be so beautiful. So *perfect*. You see it, don't you?"

"Well, I guess." I purse my lips as if I'm torn. "I guess I do."

"Of course, you do. You know that everything I did was for you and your sisters. That it was to show you how much I love you. You believe that, right, Daphne?"

Anger. So much rage fuels me now, but I can't let it blind me from what we have to do.

"Here," Horace says and waves his hand. Suddenly, there's a movie screen above his head, and he's showing us little snippets of time. Starting from when we were children.

"Look how lovely all three of you are, helping me in the garden." His face is calm and happy as he watches three girls skipping around the yard. The images change. "And here you are, outside reading your books by the trees. Spending time with *me*."

We were not. We were reading, and when we noticed he was nearby, we fled inside.

Because Horace was always creepy.

"And here." His face changes now into sinister lines as the image morphs to his lair in the bayou. So many women, tortured and terrorized. "Look at how I ended it for you. Look at the skill it took for me to make every single one of them so special. All of that blood, all of the tokens of love I saved for *you*."

"You're an evil piece of shit." My voice is as calm as his. At first, his face doesn't register what I'm saying. "And we're about to make you feel the kind of pain you inflicted on every one of those girls for all eternity."

"You little bitch!"

Now! Jackson says, and we begin the last of the spell, speaking in unison.

"With the power of the four elements in us

Horace and his evil will no longer be

Evil spirit be cast out of this plane

Trapped for all time in our vessels of pain.

As we will it, so mote it be."

We repeat the spell over and over again as we each take off our protection stones and hold them high in the air.

Horace begins to break, to fragment and shatter into tiny pieces of black mist. And as we continue to chant, he's sucked evenly into each of our stones until he's completely trapped in our hands.

The doorway closes, and we're back in the chaos and the swirling wind.

Millie waves her arms, stirring the wind at her will.

"Let's clean this up," she says with a smile. Suddenly, the shadows, the last of Horace's army, are sucked into the ground, and the portal is closed.

Under the light of the glowing full moon, eclipse finished, we stand, gasping for breath, staring at each other in the silence.

"We did it." Jackson sweeps me into his arms, and then the six of us hold one another.

"He's gone," Lucien says, relief and gratitude heavy in his voice. "Gods, we did it."

"They're not gone," Brielle says, pointing above us. "Not yet."

Jackson's parents, our grandmother, and the soldiers who came to help smile down on us. With a wave, the gateway closes.

"No one would ever believe it," Jackson says. I take his hand and look into his eyes. "Hell, I don't know if *I* believe it."

I pinch his arm.

"Okay, I believe it."

Someone behind us starts to clap, and then it spreads throughout the silent crowd.

We turn and see our friends, our loved ones,

applauding with massive smiles on their faces, all of them looking so proud. So tired.

And so completely wonderful.

Mama steps forward and hugs us close.

"I knew you could do it," she says. "Blessed be, my beautiful girls."

"We have some cleansing to do," Miss Sophia says, holding an old broom. "Our night isn't over yet."

For several hours, we sweep and clean the area. Pour more salt. Burn sage, scatter herbs, and light cleansing fires.

Until no more paranormal activity remains.

"Are you going to ask me now?" I ask Jackson after we've finished and the circle is closed. "You said you would when all of this was said and done."

He laughs and pulls me against him, kisses me gently. "And I will. But not on a battlefield. Not on *this* battlefield, anyway."

"Killjoy."

He laughs again and spins me around. "I love you, Daphne."

WE CAME BACK to Millie and Lucien's house to sleep for the night. Just the six of us. Everyone else went back to their homes, ready to sleep soundly in the knowledge that they are safe.

"I felt it," I say quietly. We're gathered in the library,

the way we've been doing for what seems like weeks now, eating breakfast and enjoying some coffee.

Goddess, I need all the coffee I can get.

And the best part is, there's no potion in it this time.

"What did you feel?" Brielle asks.

"All night long, I felt the heaviness gone. It's like a weight's been lifted. I just feel, well, weightless, I guess. Carefree. I've never known what that feels like."

Lucien reaches over to pet Sanguine, who hasn't left Millie's side since we walked in the door very early this morning.

"We did something last night that we've fought many lifetimes for," Lucien says. He has to stop and swallow the lump in his throat. "I've never grown old with Millie. I've never known what the day after the fight looks like."

"It looks like six tired people stuffing beignets into their faces," Cash says.

"What do we do with those?" I ask, pointing to the box where we stored the stones that hold Horace. "They can't stay together."

"I think each couple needs to take a vacation," Millie says. "To very different parts of the world to dispose of him so the spell can never be undone, and he can't escape. Those exact locations should never be shared outside of the person who handles the disposal."

I look immediately to Brielle, who *hates* to travel.

The shadows always torment her.

"I can do it," she says, reading my mind. "I think that's a great idea."

"It'll have to be a two-for," Jackson says. "For example, Daphne and I will have to visit two places, far apart, and leave one stone in each place."

"Exactly," Lucien says with a nod. "And I think the sooner we do it, the better."

"What will we do with all of the bloodstones and the photos he left?"

"It's already gone," Cash says simply. "No need to ask questions."

I blink at him and sip my coffee. "Sometimes, you're a scary man, Cassien."

My brother-in-law laughs and nods. "Sometimes, I guess I am."

"We've ignored our businesses for a few days." I sip the last of my coffee and then smile when it magically refills itself. I look over at Millie. "Thanks."

"You're welcome." She stretches in her chair and lazily props her feet in Lucien's lap. "I think we've all earned the right to be lazy and not get up for more coffee. And, yes, we may have been neglecting our businesses these past few days, but they'll be fine. Now that he's not a factor, everything will be just fine."

"I'm staying here today," I inform my sister. "I'm going to help you clean up from a house full of guests. Don't argue with me. It's happening."

"I'm not arguing," Millie says.

"I'm staying, too," Brielle adds.

"I'm going to go look in on Oliver and Miss Annabelle," Jackson says beside me, "but I'll be back to help."

We're quiet for a long moment, and then I hear a baby crying upstairs.

We exchange looks as the sound of a closing door also filters down.

But it isn't slammed this time.

"Life continues," Millie says softly. "I like that our house has a piece of the past still living in it. But more than that, I'm so damn grateful that we all get to live our lives and see what's in store for us next."

"Amazing things," I predict. "Many years of amazing things."

"I THINK THAT'S IT." I tap my hand against my thigh and take a good, hard look around my bedroom, just to make sure that everything I need is currently stowed in my suitcase.

We're about to leave in the morning on a week-long trip. Bora Bora will be the first stop, and then on to Australia.

Millie and Lucien left this morning for Alaska. And then they're going to spend a few days in Japan.

Brielle and Cash are on a plane right now to Peru, and then they'll spend some time in Ireland.

The stones will never be in the same place, at the same time, ever again.

"Is it weird that I miss them already?" I ask Jackson as he walks into the bedroom.

"No, you've been attached at the hip for a long time." He kisses my forehead. "Come here. I want to show you something."

"You haven't packed yet," I remind him as I follow him out of the bedroom. "Please don't be one of those travelers who packs two hours before the flight leaves. That's *so* annoying."

I stop short and feel my jaw drop.

"Wow."

Jackson smiles and pulls a long-stemmed red rose out of a vase of at least two dozen more, and holds it out for me to take. I bury my nose in it and take a long, deep breath.

"These are lovely. And you brought in food."

"I did. But before we eat..." He trails off, lowers to one knee, and pulls a ring out of the pocket of his jeans. "Daphne, you are the love of my life. My match in every way. You are the one meant for me. I want to build a long, happy life with you, sweets. I want some babies. Mostly, I just want to spend as much time as I possibly can with you, for as long as I'm on this Earth."

He licks his lips.

"Will you marry me, Daph?"

"Of course, I will." I wipe away a tear as he slips the ring on my finger, and I gasp at the sweet memories that fill my mind. "Oh, they were so happy, Jack. She loved this ring so much. It was her grandmother's. She was close to her and felt so proud to wear it. And now, I'm proud to wear it."

He stands, pulling me close. "Serendipity."

The word is whispered.

"What is?"

"Finding you, all those years ago. I wasn't looking for you, but there you were. The most amazing woman I'd ever seen. All mine."

I kiss his chin. "All yours."

He lifts me and stalks off for the bedroom.

"I thought we were going to eat!"

"We will. Later."

EPILOGUE

Miss Sophia

"Are you ready?" I smile at my friend as she zips up her bag, ready to move to her new home just down the lane from me.

Ruth has been the friend I didn't know I needed over the past several months. A constant companion and a joy to have around.

And I don't have to say goodbye to her. She'll be close, at the ready for a cup of tea or a glass of spiced wine.

Since my sister died almost two decades ago, I didn't think I'd ever feel connected to another person the way I felt connected to her.

But I was wrong.

And I'm grateful.

"I'm ready. The girls are already down there. They said they had some surprises for me."

"I'm sure they have some lovely surprises," I agree.

Lovely surprises, indeed.

We walk down the little dirt road that connects our homes. Ruth and I have enjoyed watching the progress on her little cottage, discussing colors and fabrics.

Casting spells on charms to put in the walls when the workers finished for the day.

Three cars are parked out front, and the six are sitting on the deep, wrap-around porch—the girls on the swing, in a chair, and the boys on the steps.

"What a handsome bunch they make," I say softly.

"I've never seen anything so wonderful in my life," Ruth says. "And the new house is good, too."

I smile at her, and we approach the others.

"There you are," Brielle says. "Welcome home, Mama."

"Oh, girls. All of you. It's just so wonderful. So much more than I imagined."

"Let's go inside and have a look," Jackson suggests.

They wanted us to stay away for the last phase of the build so we could see it when it was all finished.

And when we walk inside, we both gasp with joy.

Ruth cries.

I simply smile, pleased and proud of these young people and everything they've accomplished together.

The living space is full of color. A beautiful yellow velvet couch is the focal point with gem-toned pillows and throws and wood furniture. The kitchen is a dream, with plenty of counter space for Ruth to explore more of her hedgewitch affinity.

I have no doubt she'll plant gorgeous gardens, and children will play in the yard for generations to come, filling the little house with love.

"Do you like it?" Daphne asks me after we've been given the grand tour.

"Oh, darling, yes. It's absolutely perfect. Your mother will be very happy here."

"She deserves it," Millie says and hugs Ruth close.

Lucien walks up next to me and takes my hand, squeezing it.

He's my great-grandfather, this young man. And, he's my friend.

I've grieved for those we lost, loved ones who didn't have the opportunity to be here and to grow old.

And I've rejoiced for the six who prevailed, and for the lifetimes they're about to have.

They are my family.

"I'm going to make dinner for everyone," Ruth announces. "A big dinner, here in my new home."

"I think that sounds like a wonderful idea," I reply, joining in my friend's excitement. "But first, I think there are a few announcements that need to be shared."

All three sisters look at me in surprise, and then at each other.

"We're all knocked up," Brielle says with a laugh. "All three of us."

"Babies!" Ruth tears up and holds her daughter close. "My babies are having babies, Sophia."

"Yes." I look into Lucien's eyes and give him a wink.

I see their lives. All of them. Along with their children's and their children's children. I know what's to come.

There will be battles ahead. But there will also be love.

So much love.

If you or someone you know is in crisis,
call the National Suicide Prevention Lifeline
(Lifeline) at **1-800-273-TALK (8255),** or text
the Crisis Text Line (**text HELLO to 741741**). Both
services are free and available twenty-four hours a day,
seven days a week. All calls are confidential.

DON'T MISS where Bayou Magic all began with Shadows! If you're new to the series, here is a sneak peek. Shadows is available now!

SHADOWS

A Bayou Magic Novel

Shadows
A Bayou Magic Novel
By
Kristen Proby

SHADOWS

A Bayou Magic Novel

Kristen Proby

Cover Design: By Hang Le

Published by Ampersand Publishing, Inc.

Ebook ISBN 978-1-63350-047-1

A NOTE FROM THE AUTHOR

Dear Reader,

If you've read me for any length of time, you know that I love a love story. Telling love stories is what I'm most passionate about. Over the past couple of years, I've wanted to dabble in a little suspense, a little paranormal romance. I love to read this genre, and I thought it would be fun to write it. I touched on it with Mallory's story in Easy Magic, and I think you'll be pleased to see a glimpse of Mallory in this story as well.

Shadows is two years in the making. It seemed I always had other deadlines, other stories that came first. So when it was time to plot Shadows, and I sat down to write it, I was ecstatic.

And let me just tell you, it didn't disappoint.

I would like to point out that this story is darker than what I'm known for. The love story is there, of course, but there is also a quest involved that had me on the edge of my seat. Some of what's here may disturb you, as it should. We're talking about a serial killer, after all.

I hope you enjoy these sisters, their gifts, and the men who love them. This is the first of three books.

So sit back, make sure the lights are on, and let me tell you a story...

Kristen

PROLOGUE

Brielle

"Don't touch that!"

Daphne, my youngest sister, recoils from the rocking chair in the corner. It's dark under the stairs, but I know it's there.

I can see the shadow sitting in it.

The shadows are everywhere.

"Come on," I continue, gesturing for my sisters to huddle under our blanket fort with me. Shut out the shadows. The noises.

The house.

"I don't like it under here," Millie, the middle daughter says. She points her flashlight away from her face, illuminating our little haven, reflecting the quilt above us and casting everything in a red glow. We managed to sneak lots of pillows and old, ratty blankets under here. There's a storm raging tonight, and that's when it seems to be the worst.

For all of us.

We're what they call *sensitive*.

I've read books that I keep at school so our daddy doesn't see. It makes him the maddest of all.

And when Daddy's mad, we get punished.

I'm the oldest. At thirteen, I'm the one who protects my sisters from the house. From all of the bad things around us. It's always been this way. Our parents don't know. And even if they did, I'm not sure they'd care. Not really.

Because they don't believe me when I tell them about the shadows in the house.

And they don't believe Daphne when she says she sees things when she touches the old furniture.

A clap of thunder rocks the house, and Daphne lays her head in my lap, whimpering.

"I hope we don't get caught," Millie whispers. "Last time—"

"We won't," I assure. "Dad's not here, and Mama's passed out."

But, suddenly, there's a loud banging on the back door, and we all stare at each other in horror.

That entrance is only a few feet from where we're huddled under the stairs.

"She won't wake up," I whisper and pull Millie into my arms. "Please don't let her wake up."

But she does.

A few seconds later, we hear loud footsteps stomping through the house.

"I'm comin' already!" Mama yells to whoever's pounding on the door.

Soundlessly, we turn off our flashlights. Being in the dark is its own horrible torture.

But getting caught?

I don't want to even think it.

"What are you doin' here?" Mama demands after yanking open the front entry. I can feel the whoosh of air slide under the thin door of our hiding spot.

"Checkin' on you," a man says. "Storm's a doozy."

"We're fine," Mama replies. "You woke me out of a dead sleep."

"Where is he?" the man asks. I'm pretty sure it's Horace. He lives nearby and helps Mama and Daddy with things around the house.

"Gone," Mama says. "And he ain't comin' back."

I feel Daphne stiffen.

He's not coming back?

"That means you and me can—"

"It don't mean nothin'," Mama interrupts him. "Now, git. Git outta here, 'fore'n I sic the cops on you."

There are no more voices. Just a slamming door, and then Mama's feet stomping back down the hall and up the stairs to her bedroom. I hear the floorboards creak as she gets back into bed.

"Can we turn the light back on?" Millie whispers.

"Not yet," I mutter back to her. I need to make sure Mama's asleep before we turn on the lights or make any noise.

We're not supposed to be under here.

But it's the safest place in the house.

We're quiet for a long time. I run my fingers through Daphne's hair as she lays on my lap. Millie rests her head on my shoulder.

Our arms are looped around each other as the storm rages, and the house settles—more alive than ever.

"Do you hear it?" Millie asks.

The chair is rocking in the corner now, squeaking with every back and forth motion.

Footsteps upstairs. And they aren't Mama's.

"Can you tell if she's asleep?" I ask Millie.

"I don't want to reach out," she admits. Millie's psychic abilities are off the charts, even for a ten-year-old.

"Just real fast, then shut it down."

She sighs next to me and then is quiet while her mind searches the house.

"She's asleep," she whispers. "And he's here."

"Who?"

She whimpers. Daphne stirs and sits up.

"I saw him," Daphne says. "In my dream."

"Who?" I ask again and flip on my flashlight.

I don't have to ask a third time.

A new shadow is suddenly sitting with us.

"Daddy."

CHAPTER ONE

Brielle

"Hello, everyone, and welcome to my tour. I'm Brielle Landry, and I'll be your guide today. Now, I know there are roughly eleven thousand ghost tours in the French Quarter, so I thank you kindly for choosing mine."

I smile at the crowd that's gathered on the sidewalk before me. We have a group of all ages this evening, from young teenagers to middle-aged folks. There are those who want to be in the front, listening raptly. And then, of course, there are the drunk ones, who will likely be the hecklers.

"I have just a couple rules for y'all. No walking in the street. If you've been here for twenty minutes, you've already learned that drivers don't slow down, and I won't lose anyone to vehicular homicide on my tour."

The group laughs, and I continue, my eyes roaming the crowd and taking stock.

"We won't be going inside any of the beautiful buildings we'll be talking about tonight, but halfway through, we will stop at a bar to soak in some A/C and have a refreshment or two."

"Or five," Heckler Number One says, elbowing his friend.

"I'm always happy to answer questions, so don't be shy, y'hear? Now, let's get started."

I point to the big, gray building behind me. Most tours save this one for last, but not me. It's the most haunted of the group, and I want to get it over with.

Not that the rest of the tour *isn't* haunted. Ghosts are literally everywhere.

But this one? It's sinister.

I hate it.

Tour groups love it.

"This building behind me is the LaLaurie mansion," I begin. "Well, a rebuilt version of the original house, anyway. Like most buildings in the Quarter, it suffered a nasty fire. Delphine LaLaurie lived here with her third husband, Louis. She had two daughters from previous marriages. Both of her earlier husbands died early deaths."

I swallow hard as I look over at the façade. More shadows than I can count stare back at me.

"Delphine and Louis had a love for torture." The drama is thick in my New Orleans accent as I relay stories of torment, and the horrific atrocities done to the hundreds of slaves that once lived in the building behind me. "And these stories I just shared are the less horrible ones."

Several pairs of eyes whip to mine in surprise.

Including a pair of green orbs the same color as the malachite pendant I wear around my neck for protection.

I instinctively reach up and fiddle with the stone as I continue.

"Who haunts it?" someone calls out.

Who doesn't?

"One day, Delphine chased a twelve-year-old slave girl up to the roof of the building with a bullwhip. The young girl had been brushing Delphine's hair and hit a snag. She ran from the whip, and it's said she jumped to her death out of fear.

"Leah, the slave girl, is buried on the grounds of the mansion, along with countless others. When renovations were done years after Delphine and Louis fled to Paris, skeletons were found in the walls. So much death has happened here, that it wouldn't surprise me if dozens of spirits haunt the house.

"It was once owned by Nicolas Cage, but it has a different owner now. They don't offer tours."

I gesture for the group to follow me, and we continue down Royal Street.

My route through the Quarter is deliberate. I take the same path every day. There are no surprises that way.

Surprises for me are never fun.

Yes, I see shadows, but they're the same ones every time. I know where they lurk.

My hecklers turn out to be fun rather than ruining the tour for everyone else, and before long, we've stopped for our refreshments. I grab myself two bottles of water, one to drink now, and one to stow away in my bag for later.

"How do you know all this stuff?"

I turn and see those green eyes from before smiling down at me.

"I studied," I say with a grin of my own. The man is handsome as all get out, with a dimple in a cheek covered by dark stubble. But it's those eyes that draw me in. "I was a history major in college, and since I'm from this area, I've always been fascinated by local history."

"You tell a hell of a story."

"Thank you." I take a sip of my water, watching him. "Where are you from?"

"Savannah, originally."

"Another haunted city."

"They claim to be the most haunted in America."

I feel my smile turn colder. "While I've never been there, I'm sure Savannah is beautiful. But we have more dead in New Orleans than we have living. And while it's not a competition, I'd bet this city would stand up to yours any day of the week. At least, for hauntings."

"Maybe you need to visit."

Not a chance in hell.

"Maybe one day."

"I'm Cash." He holds out his hand to shake mine. His palm is warm, his grip strong.

"Brielle. But you knew that."

"You're a beautiful woman, Brielle."

"A complicated one." I wink at him, pull my hand away, and round up the troops. "Let's go, everyone. It's time for more ghost walking."

Once we're back on the sidewalk, I point to the building behind me. "This was once a boys' school. The original building burned down in the seventeen hundreds, and the boys perished in the building. It's said they still live here."

I glance back and see several small shadows looking out the windows.

"It's a hotel now, and guests have reported hearing laughter and children playing. Do you remember back in the day when we had regular film cameras?"

The older members of my group smile and nod.

"Well, back then, people would take their vacation photos. When they got home, they'd take the film in to be developed. Several vacationers reported that as they were sifting through their memories, they saw photos of them. Asleep. From above."

I glance over to see Cash raise one dark eyebrow. His dimple winks at me as he crosses his arms over his impressive chest and listens intently.

He would be less distracting if he were in the back of the group.

"So, while harmless, the boys *are* mischievous. They like to turn the channels on the TV."

"We're staying there." A woman looks up at her husband. "I'll never sleep tonight."

I laugh and, just as I turn to lead the group to the next point of interest, I falter and stop in my tracks.

A new shadow.

A new shadow.

About my height, standing on the sidewalk. I can never make out faces, but I can tell this one is turned toward me. It's a feminine spirit.

I blink quickly and try to recover so I don't alert my group to anything amiss.

A new shadow.

It's rare, even in the Quarter.

But I clear my throat and walk past the shadow to our next stop.

***

"THAT WAS *AMAZING*." A college-age girl smiles broadly and bounces on the balls of her feet. The tour ended fifteen minutes ago, but I always stay after to answer questions. "I'm Tammy. I just *loved* all of the stories. It's so interesting."

"I'm glad you enjoyed it."

"I was wondering about that Laurie house?"

"The LaLaurie?"

"Yeah. That one. Where can I learn more about her?

I mean, I know it sounds sick, but I'm fascinated by that stuff."

"Torture?"

She blushes. "History stuff. I guess it does sound awful, doesn't it?"

"There are lots of articles about Delphine online. Just Google the name, and you'll have more information than you can read. But I'll warn you, it's graphic."

"Thanks." She smiles at me, then hurries to catch up with her friend.

"People are morbidly curious," Cash says, joining me. He hung back, waiting for everyone else to ask their questions. Now, it's just the two of us.

"Always." I shudder. I know exactly what was done to those slaves.

Sometimes, the shadows talk.

"Did you have more questions, Cash?"

"One." I start to walk down the sidewalk, and he joins me. I expect him to ask about places that I didn't cover in my tour. Or maybe about the cemeteries.

Everyone always wants to know about those.

But I can't do tours there. It's too much.

Although I do have companies I can refer him to.

"What did you see?"

I stop and frown up at him. Cash is tall. Way taller than my five-foot-six height.

"Excuse me?"

"After you told the story about the kids dying in the fire, which is creepy as hell by the way, you turned, and then you stopped and went white as a sheet. You looked like you saw a ghost."

Well, I did see a ghost, Cash.

But I can't say that.

"It was great having you on the tour this evening." I smile at him and pat him on the arm. "Have a fantastic vacation. Be careful."

And with that, I hurry away, headed to the one place in the city that I'm absolutely safe.

"HELP ME PUT these chairs up, will you?"

Millie flutters around her little café, stacking chairs on tables so her night crew can come in and mop the floors.

Witches Brew will be three years old this spring, and so far, it's been a success for my younger sister. And it should be. This café is perfect for the French Quarter, from its fun name to the quirky décor and delicious menu.

Coffee served in a cauldron? Sure thing.

Want a love potion? You can order one up.

She'll also read your tarot cards if you ask nicely.

I know that tourists come in here and think it's just a fun, silly café.

But it's as real as it gets.

Millie is a gifted witch. A crazy, amazing psychic. And those love potions? Well, they're real.

She's a hedgewitch.

Or, in layman's terms, a kitchen witch.

And she's as scatterbrained and fun as she is a little scary.

I couldn't love her more.

"Whatcha doin'?" she asks as we place the chairs on the little, round tables.

"Just finished a tour. Figured I'd come in and see how business was today."

"Off the hook," she says and wipes the sweat off her brow with a towel. "And we're not even in the full swing of tourist season yet."

"Same." I smile at her. We're as different as can be. I'm dark-haired with blue eyes, and Millie is blond, tall, and has chocolate-brown eyes.

She's stunning.

"How many men did you have to chase out of here today?"

"Only one," she says, grinning. "If they'd stop ordering the love potion, I wouldn't have to chase them out at all."

"You know, you don't have to actually *give* them the potion every time. They'd never know the difference."

"I charge an extra three dollars for that brew," she says, raising her chin in the air. "And *I* would know the difference. I just need to remember to tell them not to drink it until they're outside."

I laugh and walk behind the counter that's lined with stools to help her fill the napkin dispensers.

"Aren't you exhausted?" Millie asks. "Why aren't you headed home?"

Because I saw a new shadow, and it freaked me out.

"Because I wanted to see my little sister."

"Uh-huh." She watches me closely. "I'm psychic, you know."

"You can't read me."

It's true. She can't. I have my shields up, and I'm shut down so tightly, there's no way she can read my mind. If I don't guard myself, I get inundated with spirits. Once upon a time, I thought I could escape it by moving somewhere else.

Two months in Colorado Springs proved that isn't true.

So, I came home and learned to build my walls and protect myself. Millie gave me the malachite.

So far, it's all working.

But I still see them.

"I met a guy tonight," I say casually.

"Spill it."

"His name is Cash." I wrinkle my nose. "I mean, who names their kid *Cash*?"

"Is he hot?"

"Yeah. Tall, dark, and handsome, with green eyes."

"Nice. Did he ask for your number?"

"No."

She sticks out her bottom lip in disappointment.

"He might have, but I blew him off before he could."

"Wait." She holds up a hand, her bracelets jangling. "Why would you do that?"

I take a deep breath and round the counter so I can sit on a stool. "Because he noticed something."

She raises a brow.

"I was finishing up at the Andrew Jackson Hotel."

She nods.

"As I was about to walk down the street, I turned, and there was a shadow on the sidewalk. Just standing there. I've never seen her before."

"*Her?*"

"Yeah, she was about my height. Very feminine."

"Did she say anything?"

"Not that I heard. It just threw me because you know how careful I am about my route. I don't like surprises, especially not like this. It's creepy as hell. And, yes, I know I should be used to it by now, but—"

"It's creepy, like you said." She leans on the counter and bites her lip, thinking. "It probably means that someone recently died there."

"I know that."

"And now it's a new spirit on your tour. Too bad she didn't say anything. If she did, you could add it to your show. Could be fun. *Lucy was killed in this building three days ago, and her spirit now wanders the sidewalk in front of her former home.*"

"Talk about creepy."

I sigh and run my fingers through my hair. "Did you sweep this area recently?"

"Is the floor dirty?"

I look at her as if she's being obtuse on purpose. "You know what I mean."

"It's been about a week."

"You need to do it again."

Millie frowns, looking around the space. Her shields are as strong as mine, maybe stronger because she doesn't just see the dead, she *feels* them, and that's much more dangerous.

She fiddles with the amethyst around her neck.

"What do you see?"

I narrow my eyes. "I shouldn't tell you."

"I don't want to look, Bri. I dropped my guard for just a second earlier and was slammed with the pervy thoughts of a nineteen-year-old college kid who couldn't take his eyes off my ass. So, just tell me. Is it the little girl again?"

"Yeah. And she brought a friend." I reach over to take my sister's hand. "Don't drop your shields anymore, Mill. Not for a minute. *Ever.* I know we live and work here in the Quarter because it's where we make our living, but it could really hurt us."

"I know."

"I couldn't bear it if I lost you, too."

She shakes her head. "You didn't lose Daphne."

"She's not speaking to me."

"Because you're both stubborn as hell, and you need to get over it."

"You always were the peacekeeper."

"That's what being the middle child does for you, it literally puts you in the middle. I love you both. Now, snap out of it and just call her."

"I will."

"Liar."

I laugh and then frown when a third shadow appears. It looks just like the one from the sidewalk.

"What is it?"

"You need to cleanse this place. I think all of the different auras coming in and out of here all day is leaving some residual energy behind."

"I'll do it tonight before I leave. I'm also going to make you something special, so don't move that butt from that seat."

"You're bossy."

"And sassy." She winks as she fills a stainless-steel shaker with all kinds of things that I don't recognize.

This is not my area of expertise.

I can talk about the history of New Orleans all day.

My sister, however, mixes potions and casts spells.

She's gifted. She learned with some of the most powerful witches in the world, right here in New Orleans.

"How is Miss Sophia?" I ask, making Millie smile.

"She's amazing. She said to tell you hello. And to guard yourself." Millie frowns. "I forgot to pass that along. But she also said that you need to be strong regarding what's to come."

"What's that mean? What's coming?"

"She didn't say."

"She always leaves the most important parts out."

Millie pours the concoction into a glass and slides it over to me.

"No love potion, right?"

"No. It's a shielding potion. For protection."

I sniff it. "Smells like strawberries." I take a sip and smile in surprise. "Wow, it's like a milkshake."

"Helps it go down easier," she says with a wink. "Come back tomorrow, and I'll make you another."

"I'll gain ten pounds." I take another sip. "But I don't think I care. Wait, can you just do some kind of spell to take the calories out?"

"Sorry." She giggles and drinks the rest of the drink herself. "If I could do that, I'd be super-rich."

I finish my drink, and after I help Millie wash my glass and tidy up from the impromptu beverage, I wave goodbye to her.

"Be careful," she says before closing the door.

I'm always careful.

I take the same path from her place to mine, every single time. So far, I haven't seen any shadows on this route, and that makes me happy. The bars and clubs are hopping, full of tourists drinking and dancing. The French Quarter hums with energy, no matter the time of day.

I glance to my right just before I cross the street that leads several more blocks to where my apartment is, and am surprised to see Cash standing on the sidewalk, leaning against a pole.

"Are you following me?" I ask.

"No, ma'am," he says with an easy smile. "It seems I'm just destined to run into you. Can't say that I mind."

I smile back at him, regretting the way I brushed him off earlier.

"Well, then, perhaps I'll run into you again."

"I do hope so." He winks, and I hurry along to my apartment.

I round the corner of my block and stop in my tracks.

"Who are you?"

There's no answer, but I know it's the same shadow from the sidewalk and from Millie's café.

No shadows have ever followed me before.

Why now?

NEWSLETTER SIGN UP

I hope you enjoyed reading this story as much as I enjoyed writing it! For upcoming book news, be sure to join my newsletter! I promise I will only send you news-filled mail, and none of the spam. You can sign up here:

https://mailchi.mp/kristenproby.com/
newsletter-sign-up

ALSO BY KRISTEN PROBY:

Other Books by Kristen Proby

The With Me In Seattle Series

Come Away With Me
Under The Mistletoe With Me
Fight With Me
Play With Me
Rock With Me
Safe With Me
Tied With Me
Breathe With Me
Forever With Me
Stay With Me
Indulge With Me
Love With Me
Dance With Me

Dream With Me

You Belong With Me

Imagine With Me

Shine With Me

Escape With Me

Flirt With Me

Check out the full series here: https://www.
kristenprobyauthor.com/with-me-in-seattle

The Big Sky Universe

Love Under the Big Sky

Loving Cara

Seducing Lauren

Falling for Jillian

Saving Grace

The Big Sky

Charming Hannah

Kissing Jenna

Waiting for Willa

Soaring With Fallon

Big Sky Royal

Enchanting Sebastian

Enticing Liam

Taunting Callum

Heroes of Big Sky
Honor
Courage

Check out the full Big Sky universe here: https://
www.kristenprobyauthor.com/under-the-big-sky

Bayou Magic
Shadows
Spells
Serendipity

Check out the full series here: https://www.
kristenprobyauthor.com/bayou-magic

The Romancing Manhattan Series

All the Way
All it Takes
After All

Check out the full series here: https://www.
kristenprobyauthor.com/romancing-manhattan

The Boudreaux Series

Easy Love
Easy Charm
Easy Melody

Easy Kisses

Easy Magic

Easy Fortune

Easy Nights

Check out the full series here: https://www.
kristenprobyauthor.com/boudreaux

The Fusion Series

Listen to Me

Close to You

Blush for Me

The Beauty of Us

Savor You

Check out the full series here: https://www.
kristenprobyauthor.com/fusion

From 1001 Dark Nights

Easy With You

Easy For Keeps

No Reservations

Tempting Brooke

Wonder With Me

Shine With Me

Kristen Proby's Crossover Collection

Soaring with Fallon, A Big Sky Novel

Wicked Force: A Wicked Horse Vegas/Big Sky Novella
By Sawyer Bennett

All Stars Fall: A Seaside Pictures/Big Sky Novella
By Rachel Van Dyken

Hold On: A Play On/Big Sky Novella
By Samantha Young

Worth Fighting For: A Warrior Fight Club/Big Sky
Novella
By Laura Kaye

Crazy Imperfect Love: A Dirty Dicks/Big Sky Novella
By K.L. Grayson

Nothing Without You: A Forever Yours/Big Sky Novella
By Monica Murphy

Check out the entire Crossover Collection here:

https://www.kristenprobyauthor.com/kristen-proby-crossover-collection

ABOUT THE AUTHOR

Kristen Proby has published more than fifty titles, many of which have hit the USA Today, New York Times and Wall Street Journal Bestsellers lists.

Kristen and her husband, John, make their home in her hometown of Whitefish, Montana with their two cats and dog.

facebook.com/booksbykristenproby

instagram.com/kristenproby

bookbub.com/profile/kristen-proby

goodreads.com/kristenproby

Made in the USA
Monee, IL
21 October 2021

80421052R00194